An Unexpected Temptation

The Townsbridges, Volume 6

Sophie Barnes

Published by Sophie Barnes, 2020.

By Sophie Barnes
Novels

The Formidable Earl
Her Seafaring Scoundrel
The Forgotten Duke
More Than A Rogue
The Infamous Duchess
No Ordinary Duke
The Illegitimate Duke
The Girl Who Stepped Into The Past
The Duke of Her Desire
Christmas at Thorncliff Manor
A Most Unlikely Duke
His Scandalous Kiss
The Earl's Complete Surrender
Lady Sarah's Sinful Desires
The Danger in Tempting an Earl
The Scandal in Kissing an Heir
The Trouble with Being a Duke
The Secret Life of Lady Lucinda
There's Something About Lady Mary
Lady Alexandra's Excellent Adventure

How Miss Rutherford Got Her Groove Back

Novellas

An Unexpected Temptation
A Duke for Miss Townsbridge
Falling For Mr. Townsbridge
Lady Abigail's Perfect Romance
When Love Leads To Scandal
Miss Compton's Christmas Romance
The Duke Who Came To Town
The Earl Who Loved Her
The Governess Who Captured His Heart
Mistletoe Magic (from Five Golden Rings: A Christmas Collection)

Chapter One

BALANCING AT THE EDGE of the sofa, Athena waited for her four-year-old niece, Lilly, to make her next move.

"Come on," Lilly's older brother, Lucas, said. "You're taking forever."

"It's hard," Lilly said. She stared at the low stool she was meant to get onto next. "My legs are too short."

Athena had deliberately placed the furniture with this in mind. She knew Lilly could make the jump with ease, but after misjudging the distance between two stone benches in Hyde Park a few weeks earlier, the girl was fearful of falling and getting hurt once more. Sympathizing, Athena grabbed a throw cushion and tossed it onto the floor. It landed between Lilly's chair and the stool.

Lucas jerked toward her with a glare. "That's cheating."

"Would you rather your sister be eaten by crocodiles?" Athena asked. Lilly hopped down onto the cushion, freeing up the chair so Athena could move forward.

"No," Lucas grumbled. "But she could have made that jump. And now she's about to grab the treasure."

"Unless you're able to reach it first," Athena told him slyly.

"Not possible," Lilly said with confidence.

"What did I say at the very beginning," Athena asked, "when you insisted there were no crocodiles in England?"

"To use our imagination," Lucas said. His eyes suddenly widened. He seemed to study his surroundings with greater care. A grin widened his mouth as he eyed the folded blanket hanging over the back of the loveseat. "I'm making a bridge."

"You can't," Lilly said. She turned to Athena. "Can he?"

"I can't very well stop him after I made an island pop out of nowhere for you."

"I'd rather play hide and go seek," Lilly grumbled. She crossed her arms and pouted while her brother triumphantly claimed the biscuit tin at the center of the room.

"We can do that next," Athena said. "After you have survived the pit of doom."

Lilly blew out a breath and leapt across to where her brother stood. Athena jumped forward as well, landing on the stool as the door to the parlor swung open.

"What on earth is going on in here?" Athena's mother, Viscountess Roxley, asked. Mouth agape, she stared at Athena. As it turned out, she was not alone. The rest of the house party stood immediately behind her.

"Playing," Athena told the assembled group. She and her entire family had been invited to spend the second two weeks of December at the Marquess and Marchioness of Foxborough's estate. The Foxboroughs's daughter, Abigail, had married Athena's brother James three years prior.

"That is what one does in the nursery, Athena. Not," her mother informed her, "in the parlor belonging to one's host and hostess."

"I'm sorry," Athena said, "but the nursery furniture isn't very conducive to jungle adventures."

"It's quite all right," Lady Foxborough said with a slight frown. "I'm sure we can put the room to rights quickly enough if we all lend a hand."

"William," Athena's oldest brother, Charles, told their sibling. "Help me move the sofa, would you?"

Athena hopped off the stool and picked up the blanket Lucas had used as a bridge. She proceeded to fold it.

"Do we still get our biscuits?" Lucas asked while hugging the tin.

"Yes," Athena assured him, "but you may have to share with a lot more people now. Unless you make a hasty escape."

Lucas gave the doorway a quick glance, then grabbed his sister's hand and promptly took off, with Lilly tripping and squealing behind him.

"Honestly," Athena's mother sighed. "Could you not try to set a better example for them?"

Athena shrugged. "They can learn about rules and decorum from everyone else. From me, however, they shall learn how to have fun."

"Which is why we left them in your care in the first place," Charles's wife, Bethany, told Athena with a twinkle in her eyes.

"And we have every intention of doing the same with Benedict once he's old enough," Abigail said. "So I hope this won't be the only time we're tidying up this room."

Athena shared a look with her mother. The lady's features softened until she allowed a smile. Athena knew she'd only chided her because she believed it was her responsibility to do so, not because she actually minded the ruckus. If anything,

Lord and Lady Roxley both welcomed the boisterousness their grandchildren provided. As they put it, it made them feel young again. But they were very aware that this was not a view shared by all since most members of the upper class preferred to have their children hidden away and cared for by governesses.

"Hopefully, the weather tomorrow will be clear so we can get the children outside," Charles said once all the furniture had been put back in its proper spot and everyone comfortably seated. "A long walk and some fresh air would be wonderful for them."

A maid arrived with a tray, allowing tea to be served. Athena took a soothing sip while the conversation ensued around her. She loved that they'd all been gathered in this way. With her sister, Sarah, married off to the Duke of Brunswick in October, she'd experienced a void in her life she'd not been prepared for. All too often, she found herself reflecting on how things used to be before her siblings had moved out of Townsbridge House. There had been laughter and love, constant chatter, footsteps moving across the floors, the sound of games being played.

Now there was too much silence, and Athena longed to escape it, to carve out moments for herself in which she could recreate what she missed. Only there was no going back, just forward, and the future that spanned before her looked mighty lonely.

Of course, the solution would be to marry and have a hoard of children of her own. The only problem with this was that she wasn't sure she'd ever make a match for herself, as evidenced by her lack of suitors. No man wanted to touch a woman as daring or unpredictable as she. They couldn't accept the scandal she'd caused at the age of fourteen when she'd stood up in church and informed everyone that Bethany loved Charles rather than the man she'd been in the process of marrying.

Mayhem had ensued and Athena's reputation had suffered irreparable damage. But, she mused, she would do the same thing again in a heartbeat. For if there was one thing she could not abide, it was the idea of people sacrificing their happiness for fear of causing a scandal. As far as she was concerned, there was only one life, one chance to get it all right. Why waste that on making oneself deliberately miserable for the sole purpose of appeasing others?

"We have the holiday dance at the assembly hall of course, but if you like we could arrange a ball here as well," Lady Foxborough said, snapping Athena out of her reverie. "There are a few families in the area we could invite. A couple even have young men of marriageable age."

"Really?" Athena's mother murmured with far too much interest for Athena's liking.

"Plotting the next match already?" Athena's father asked with the resignation of a man who'd long since realized there was no point in trying to dissuade his wife from her goals. "You don't waste any time, do you, dear?"

"I see no reason to," Athena's mother said.

"How about the fact that Sarah was allowed to wait until she was two-and-twenty before she married?" Athena asked. In truth, she wouldn't mind finding a man with whom she could fall in love sooner rather than later, she simply didn't believe it was likely to happen and had no desire to suffer the torture of being paraded about. "I should be permitted to do the same."

"All things considered, I think it would be best if we began showing you off to your best advantage as soon as possible," her mother argued. "You've many excellent qualities, Athena. I'd like to remind people of that so they can start viewing you in a different light."

In other words, her mother expected her road to the altar to be a lengthy one involving a shift in public opinion. No time to waste then. She allowed herself an inward groan and took another sip of her tea.

"Mama has the right of it," William said. "And a ball would be a great deal of fun."

"There's just one catch," Lord Foxborough said, cutting a stern look at his wife. "Protocol would require us to invite the Marquess of Darlington, and I'm not sure how any of you would feel about that."

Athena's hand shook in response to the name. Hot tea fell against her thigh. Robert Carlisle had been the Earl of Langdon when she'd last seen him. Although things had ended badly between them, she'd been sorry to hear of his father's passing. Athena darted a look in Charles's direction. He and Bethany had both gone utterly still.

"I forgot he had property in this area," Athena's father finally said.

"I've not spoken to him in six years. Not since I left him at that inn where I found him after..." Charles cleared his throat and clasped his wife's hand.

Athena returned her teacup to its saucer with a clatter. "I should like a chance to apologize to him."

"No." The word was unanimously spoken by her parents and siblings alike.

"But—"

"Darlington was furious after what happened." Charles's voice was strained with regret. "He made it very clear to me there was nothing more to be said between us."

"Nevertheless, I would like a chance to explain myself to him directly." What she was truly after was his forgiveness. Darlington had been Charles's friend. She'd known him most of her life and while he'd been wrong for Bethany, she could not deny the guilt she still felt over how she'd upended his life. "It would mean a great deal."

"I'm sorry," Charles said. A brief silence followed before he confessed. "I made repeated attempts to apologize to him on all our behalves. I wrote him letters, Athena, and he responded once, in a manner I cannot repeat with ladies present. His words were extremely harsh, especially those directed at you. And while I've no doubt he was foxed beyond reason when he penned the missive, I cannot excuse such behavior."

"Not even when we are the ones who drove him to it?" Athena asked. She held Charles's gaze. "Out of everyone who has criticized me over the years for the part I played in your marriage to Bethany, he is the one with the most right."

"You're not wrong," Athena's father said, "but there are instances when it is wisest to leave the past alone and move on. It is my opinion that this is such an instance. Our goal right now is to see you settled, not to ruin your chances further by reminding everyone of what happened, and yes, they will be reminded the moment they see you and Darlington in the same room."

"So then I gather we ought to avoid a ball?" Lady Foxborough asked.

"What about the dance at the assembly hall?" Bethany asked. "Is there any chance Darlington might show up there?"

"No," Lady Foxborough said. "The marquess, as I understand it, does not go out at all."

"So then?" Athena prompted. "Why not invite him if you know he'll stay away."

"I fear he would not." Lady Foxborough reached for her teacup while Athena tried to make sense of what she was being told. "The assembly hall functions are free from obligation, but if we, the Marquess and Marchioness of Foxborough, were to ask another peer to join us for a formal event, I believe he would feel duty-bound to attend, so as not to cause offense."

Athena sank back against the sofa with a sigh. What foolish nonsense. The Foxboroughs could not host a ball because to do so they would have to invite a man who did not wish to attend but would have to do so simply for the sake of appeasing a group of people who did not want him there. Once again, she was reminded of how ridiculous Society was.

She glanced at the beveled glass windows, wet with rain. For six years she'd dreamed of running into Darlington, of voicing her regrets and wishing him well. In all her imaginings, he'd refuse to listen at first, but would relent when she persisted. Eventually, he'd tell her he understood, that it was all right, and that what had happened was for the best.

The only problem was, the marquess had cut all ties with her family and remained absent from Town. She'd had no chance to approach him – no opportunity to make amends. Until now.

Her pulse quickened. She wondered how far away his estate might be. If the Foxboroughs felt they had to invite him to an evening affair in the winter, he must be quite close – at least within an hour's drive by carriage. Pressing her lips together, she considered those around her. None would provide her with the directions she required.

Perhaps it was just as well. Athena picked up a biscuit and bit into it with a sigh. She knew herself well enough to realize it was probably a foolish idea – the sort of idea best scrapped before it fully formed and began to grow roots in her brain.

But when she got up the following morning after a restless night of contemplation, she accepted what had to be done. If she was to find true happiness, she would have to make peace with the man she'd hurt. It was the only way forward.

Resolved, she called for her maid to help her dress. "I need to know how to get to the Marquess of Darlington's estate. Can you please find out for me, Mary?"

The maid was silent a moment before she said, "Of course, miss, but if you're thinking of going there, I ought to caution you against it."

"Duly noted," Athena said.

"It really wouldn't be wise."

"You're probably right, but it's one of those things I cannot *not* do."

Mary finished fastening the back of Athena's gown. "Very well, but at least allow me to accompany you."

"Thank you, but you must stay here and cover for me. I'll be as quick as I can. I promise." It took a few more added pleas to acquire Mary's full cooperation, upon which Athena went to breakfast with her family.

"It's still cloudy, but at least the rain has stopped," Abigail said. "We could take a walk to the village and shop for

Christmas gifts. I'm sure Lilly and Lucas would love the chance to purchase a few things for their parents with their aunts' and uncles' help."

"An excellent idea," James said with a loving smile aimed at his wife.

Everyone else agreed.

"There's an excellent tea shop where we can stop for pie," Lady Foxborough said. "It's the perfect place for us to warm up with refreshments."

"It sounds wonderful," Athena said, deliberately softening her voice to a weaker tone than usual, "but I am hoping I can be excused."

"Excused?" Her mother gave her a baffled look. "You love fresh air and long walks, not to mention the chance to chase your niece and nephew along a country road."

"True." Indeed, she would miss that part a great deal. "Unfortunately, I woke with a terrible headache. I think I would be better off staying here and getting some rest."

"Oh." Her mother glanced about as if unsure of what else to say, except, "Of course."

One hour later, Athena watched from her bedchamber window as her family set off on their walk. Bundled up with hats, scarves, and mittens, Lilly and Lucas skipped ahead until they reached the large stones at the edge of the driveway. Athena smiled when they scampered up onto them, and Charles hurried over to give them a hand for support.

Stepping back, she went to her wardrobe and sought out her breeches. She always wore them under her skirts when she went outside in the winter. They added an extra layer of warmth she'd never been able to garner from stockings alone.

And since she favored riding astride over using a sidesaddle, they also helped avoid chafing.

Donning a heavy wool cloak and gloves, Athena listened to Mary while she told her how to reach Lord Darlington's estate, then went to the stables and picked out a horse. Ten minutes later, she was galloping across the fields, determined to accomplish her task before anyone realized she'd even been gone.

ROBERT CARLISLE, ONCE the Earl of Langdon, now the Marquess of Darlington, stared at the numbers he'd tallied and smiled. Finally. After six long years of hard work, the investments he'd made were starting to turn a profit. Closing the ledger, he sank back in his armchair and rubbed the bridge of his nose. Lord, he was tired, but it seemed his dedication had paid off.

Rising, he went to pour himself a brandy. It wasn't even noon yet, but damn if a celebration of sorts wasn't in order. The liquid trickled into his tumbler with a rippling effect that tempted him as much as the brandy's golden color. Warmth seeped into his veins as he drank, instilling a calm he'd not known in ages.

His life, some might say, had been blessed with privilege. Most would raise their eyebrows at him if he spoke a single complaint. After all, there were men who were far worse off. This was indisputable. And yet, he did not think himself blessed with good fortune. Quite the opposite, in fact.

Robert took another blissful sip of his drink.

First, his fiancée, Charlotte Walker, had run off with his cousin. A few years later, his good friend Charles Townsbridge – nay, Charles's sister, Athena – had broken up his wedding at the church in front of all creation, claiming his bride loved Charles instead. And then, when Robert's life was finally starting to gain a bit of equilibrium again, his father had died, leaving behind a crushing amount of debt. His own financial situation at the time had not been the best, so the last thing he'd needed was more worry.

At least his financial troubles were starting to ease a little. As for the rest…

According to what he'd learned, Charlotte was desperately unhappy with a husband who liked to drown himself in a bottle of brandy each evening. Robert couldn't say he was sorry to hear it. She'd treated him abominably.

Charles Townsbridge, on the other hand, was happily married. And while Robert didn't exactly harbor ill will toward him or his wife, Bethany, a part of him envied the perfect life they'd made for themselves. It really wasn't fair that he, who'd been wronged, had suffered the most.

Crossing to the window, he glanced out at the dreary landscape, at the leafless branches reaching toward the sky as if begging for spring to dress them. Bethany should have been his. He'd met her first, proposed, and gained her hand. Hell, he'd stood with her before the priest on the very cusp of making her his when Athena, that blasted hoyden of a child, had ruined it all. She might have meant well, but that didn't change the fact that she'd made a mockery of him. The articles and caricatures he'd seen in the papers for several weeks after confirmed it. No experience had ever been more emasculating. Fresh on the heels of Charlotte's betrayal, the situation had been insufferable to say the least.

Robert blew out his breath and forced an inner calm upon himself. This was all in the past. Six years lay between the man he'd been then and the one he was now. He'd come to terms with what had happened, had finally moved on.

Perhaps, he considered while watching a cluster of birds scatter across the greying sky, it was time to start thinking of marriage once more. A nerve ticked in his jaw at the thought. Very well. Perhaps he'd wait a while yet.

A knock sounded at the door.

"Enter!" Robert turned to face his butler with the impatience of a man who wished to be left alone. "Yes?"

"You have a visitor, my lord," Dartwood said in an even tone. He raised his chin ever so slightly, then added, "She says her name is Miss Athena Townsbridge."

Robert's grip tightened on his glass. Every muscle in his shoulders and back knotted in defiance. His jaw clenched. What the hell was she doing here?

"Offer her some refreshments. Then send her on her way." He turned his back on Dartwood. "Let me know when she's gone."

"Very well, my lord." The door closed with a snick.

Robert closed his eyes and forced himself to exhale a slow breath. Between the burden of holding onto his properties, taking care of his tenants, and figuring out how to pay the taxes and his servants' wages, the very last thing he needed was for that Townsbridge brat to show up and complicate things even further. Good God! He inhaled slowly – deep calming breaths to undo the tension and infuse some calm – and exhaled.

Athena had been what, three years of age the first time he'd met her? He'd been thirteen. It had been summer and Charles had invited him home to visit his family for the holidays. Robert had joined Charles on several similar occasions in the years that followed. He remembered Athena whispering secrets in her older sister, Sarah's, ear. She'd balanced along the top of the property fence when she was eleven. One day, she'd arrived for supper covered in mud because of a tumble she'd taken. At twelve she'd harpooned a fish using a spear she'd whittled. Her triumphant smile from that long ago day was still branded in his mind.

He shook his head. Athena Townsbridge was a tempestuous handful, as evidenced by her lack of regard for propriety. *Bethany and Charles are in love with each other, but they are prepared to sacrifice their happiness for you.* Her words had been loud and clear, unwaveringly bold. He couldn't remember much from the moments that followed, except for her face, her mouth set in a firm line, eyes blazing with fierce determination.

And then he'd punched Charles, because he sure as hell couldn't punch Athena.

Another knock sounded at the door.

"Yes?"

"My apologies, my lord," Dartwood said, "but the lady refuses to leave without having met with you first."

Damn.

Robert downed the rest of his drink and set his tumbler aside with a clank. "Have her make an appointment then, for the day after never."

Dartwood made a choked sort of sound. Robert raised an eyebrow.

"I shall pass the message along," Dartwood said and departed once more. He returned ten minutes later looking more perplexed than Robert had ever seen him. "My lord. It would appear that the lady refuses to budge."

"What are you talking about?"

"She will not leave her chair."

"Oh, for God's sake."

"Shall I ask the footmen to carry her outside?"

Robert scrubbed his palm across his brow. Why couldn't his life be simple and free from complications? Why did Athena Townsbridge, of all women in the entire world, have to be the very one who decided to pay him a visit?

Aware of the awkward position she'd placed his butler in and somewhat vexed on Dartwood's behalf, Robert straightened his spine and squared his shoulders. Fine. He'd deal with the impossible chit himself.

Striding past his butler, Robert entered the hallway and made his way toward the parlor at a clipped pace. So, Athena thought she could force him to listen to her, did she? She thought she could bully his servants into compliance? After everything she'd put him through, she had some bloody nerve. He muttered a curse. If only he had a secretary and a valet to help make her leave, but the recent state of his finances had unfortunately forced him to be frugal.

Arriving at the door he sought, he flung it open with such force he heard the wood crack. "Christ almighty," he blurted in pure frustration, "your childish behavior is not to be borne."

"It is good to see you too, Robert." Athena rose from her seat like a queen about to bestow a knighthood upon her loyal subject.

She was different than how he remembered.

Robert's muscles flexed. He blinked.

When he'd last seen her she'd been a child – a bratty hoyden who ran completely wild. That was how he remembered her. It was the image he had retained inside his head for six years whenever he'd thought of her. He hardly knew what to say. Apparently, the plain girl he'd once known had transformed into a beautiful young lady.

Irritation flared. It was just like her to come here like this and shock the hell out of him. He glanced around. "Where is your chaperone?"

"I chose not to bring one."

Of course. She was just as mad as ever.

"I believe my butler told you to leave." Robert winced in response to the harsh sound of his voice and the rudeness with which he'd spoken, but frankly, he felt like his head was on backward right now.

"He did."

"And rather than heed him, you chose to set up camp with the same degree of stubbornness you've always applied to everything." He snorted. "By God, you haven't changed one bit, have you?" *Only in appearance.*

Athena raised her chin. "I like to think I've grown up."

Robert stared at her.

Gone were the chubby facial features of her adolescence, replaced by high cheekbones and a delicate jawline. The shapeless figure he recalled her having, not dissimilar to that of a boy, had been exchanged with luscious curves – with hips that flared out from her waist, and breasts... Good God. Athena Townsbridge had breasts – a most generous pair – and he was now gaping at them as if he'd never seen such an anatomical feature before.

He sucked in a breath and forced himself to raise his gaze to the vicinity of her eyes. This was wrong. So very horribly wrong. He'd accused her of being childish, but there was nothing remotely childish about her anymore. She was a woman – a very attractive one at that. He had to get her out of his house at once.

"So you have. Apparently without improving your manners." Lord help him, he'd be ready for Bedlam after this visit. Especially if she continued watching him as she did, from behind a curtain of thick black lashes, eyes bright with vitality. Her rosy lips curved ever so gently into the sort of cheeky devil-may-care smirk he feared would haunt his dreams later. *Christ have mercy*. He steeled himself. "Once again, you have chosen to ignore my wishes."

"Only because I desire to speak with you," she said. "Or was that part not clear?"

Her voice was no longer as squeaky as he remembered, but rather soft and... Robert struggled to find the right word and could only come up with *sultry*. Which did not bode well at all. Annoyed with her for disturbing his peace and with himself for noticing her feminine assets, he gestured toward her with impatience. "Go on then. Say your piece, if you must, so I can get back to work."

Chapter Two

ATHENA'S HEART HAMMERED wildly against her breast. Not only because she'd been given a chance, but because of the man who stood before her. Taller than she recalled, with a pair of broad shoulders that almost spanned the width of the doorway behind him, he looked like the very embodiment of masculine strength and power. The hair, she noted, was still the same – a blend of bronze and gold – but it was cut in a shorter style now. A pair of hard, sky-blue eyes stared back at her from beneath a furrowed brow. His mouth was set in a firm line of displeasure. And yet, in spite of all this, she had the most bizarre urge to reach out and trace her fingertips over his unshaven jawline. The bristly texture there tempted her in the same way a bolt of slippery silk would at the milliners – she simply had to know what it felt like against her skin.

Frowning on account of her foolishness, Athena glanced at the chair she'd occupied until his arrival. "Shall we sit?"

"You may do as you wish," he said. "I prefer to remain standing."

Well, she wasn't about to let him tower over her any more than he already did. She clasped her hands together and raised her chin while doing her best to ignore the churning of her stomach. She'd never been nervous before. Not ever. And yet, there was no denying the apprehension that now assailed her.

Swallowing, Athena took a fortifying breath and said, "I owe you an apology."

He stared at her as if she were daft.

"For the manner in which I behaved toward you six years ago," she added, as if that part required explanation.

A nerve ticked at the edge of his jaw. "If that is all, I shall have my butler show you out. Again."

The churning in her stomach fanned outward until it collided with her frantic heartbeats. Her words seemed to fall on deaf ears and she could not allow that. She needed him to assuage her guilt.

Desperate, she took a step forward. "My sole intention was to ensure my brother's happiness, and in so doing, I fear I caused a great deal of damage. For which I am truly sorry. Robert, I—"

"Lord Darlington, if you please."

"Of course." She bit her lip. His eyes darkened. A tremor raked her spine. "Please. Forgive me."

"Forgive you?" A snort of derision filled the air. "You stood up in church, before one and all, and announced that the woman I was about to marry loved someone else – that she preferred another man to me and that the only reason I'd not been informed was for the sake of sparing my feelings."

"I'm sorry."

"You're sorry." He leaned forward with flint in his eyes, piercing her to her very soul. "Forget the fact that hundreds of pounds in wedding expenses were wasted. Or that it was to be a marriage based solely on convenience. You ridiculed me, made a mockery of my reputation, and ensured no other woman of noble birth would ever wish to come within ten paces of me. I was scorned because of you, laughed at. And while I can appreciate the fact that you were but fourteen years of age with nothing but romantic notions filling your brain and that you were courageous enough to do what your brother should have done sooner, I cannot forgive you."

Athena could only blink in response at the violent anger to which she'd become a witness. She'd ruined his life. There was no getting past that. "Marriage is forever. Would you really wish to be tied to a woman who loved someone else?"

He leaned back, closed his eyes briefly, and finally shook his head before pinning her once again with the fierce intensity of his gaze. "It no longer matters."

"It does to me."

A humorless laugh answered her comment. "Does the guilt haunt your days, Miss Townsbridge? Does it keep you from sleep at night?"

She crossed her arms and firmed her jaw against his mocking tone. "You were a good family friend. Charles was prepared to sacrifice his own happiness for you. So was Bethany. They would both have been miserable, while you..."

"Yes?"

She glared back at him. "Would you rather be blind, my lord? Or do you prefer to see?"

He held her gaze for a long, hard moment before he finally swung away and strode to the door. "This conversation is over, Miss Townsbridge. I'll thank you never to call upon me again."

Athena stared at his retreating form until he vanished from sight. A quivering breath stole its way past her lips.

Weak-legged, she sank onto the chair behind her. Goodness gracious. The perfectly polished, well-mannered gentleman she'd once known had been transformed into an ill-bred heathen. Robert Carlisle was no longer the good-natured man notorious for his ready smiles and kind remarks. He was a thunderstorm to be reckoned with, and she'd not been prepared for that.

Her fault, of course. Everything was her fault. She had to do better – try harder – to put it to rights. Bolstering herself, she got back onto her feet, clenched her fists and marched out into the hallway.

"Miss Townsbridge," the butler said as he approached her. "I understand you are leaving."

The hell she was. She forced a smile. "Not quite."

The butler's face fell. "I, um...see."

She stormed past him. "Where is his lordship?"

"Miss Townsbridge, you cannot mean to—"

She flung a door open on her right. A study came into view. Athena cast a quick glance at the desk, noted the open ledger there, and smiled. It pleased her to know that in spite of the somewhat chaotic appearance he'd put on display for her in the parlor, Darlington was keeping order in his accounts.

Continuing her search for the master of the manor, Athena swept toward the next door.

"Miss Townsbridge," the butler said with greater insistence. "Your behavior is not the least bit appropriate."

She scoffed. As if this wasn't what she'd been hearing most of her life. Her hand reached forward to push down the handle. The door swung open and Darlington, looking mighty irate, scowled at her from his position at the head of the dining room table.

"I thought I told you to leave," he said as he pushed back his chair and stood.

"In a manner of speaking," she agreed as she entered the room. A dismal shade of grey covered the walls – a suitable hue to match the mood of their recent conversation.

"My apologies, my lord," the butler spoke from behind Athena. "I did try to stop her from interrupting your luncheon."

"I could use a bit of sustenance before I go," Athena said. It was only half past twelve. If she left by one o'clock she could still return to Foxborough Hall with time to spare before her family returned from the village. She was certain of it.

Darlington closed his eyes briefly as if in prayer, then motioned to his butler. "Please prepare another place setting for Miss Townsbridge."

"Yes, my lord." The butler hastened to do as asked.

Darlington gave Athena a grim look. "Once you have eaten, you will go. Is that understood?"

"Yes. Thank you."

He dipped his head and waited for her to claim her seat opposite him before resuming his own. A footman filled her glass with wine. Another brought her a plate filled with soggy looking vegetables and fried sausages along with a hunk of bread. Not exactly the most appealing fare, but certainly good enough to buy her more time.

Athena scooped up some vegetables and ate. They were as bland as they appeared. She took a sip of her wine, which was surprisingly good by contrast. "I would like to make amends."

"You live in a dream world, Miss Townsbridge."

She bristled at that but forced herself not to get riled up. If she was to help him, she'd have to keep a cool head. "You said your reputation was ruined by what I did, that you were ridiculed and that no woman of breeding would ever—"

"I know what I said," he snapped.

"Right. Of course you do." She began cutting her sausage into tiny pieces. The part about his reputation might be true, but the rest... Taking another bite, she considered him with discretion. No man she'd ever seen had looked more masculine than the one whose company she presently shared. As for no woman of breeding wanting him near her, that simply couldn't be true when she herself had the strangest yearning for his attention. She took another sip of her wine, for fortification. "What if I'm able to restore your reputation?"

"No."

"Why not?"

"Because the last thing I want is for you to involve yourself further in my life."

It was a fair point even if it did sting a bit. "My family is not a stranger to scandal. If you have kept abreast of the news, you will know the Townsbridges have suffered through several stormy incidents over the years." When he snorted in response she said, "After the episode involving Charles and Bethany, there was James. He accidentally compromised Abigail, who was later abducted on her way to their wedding. Then there was William who married Mama's cook. And finally, Sarah turned down a duke's proposal in public only to change her mind later. Each case invited gossip, some nastier than the rest, but we Townsbridges got through it all by sticking together."

"What is your point?"

"You need allies, my lord, and that is something I can provide."

He stared at her. "You want me to crawl back to your family and beg them for help?"

"No, I—"

"Absolutely not," he thundered. Rising, he glanced at her plate, then at the window. "Are you almost finished? It is starting to snow and the very last thing I desire is for you to get stuck here."

She didn't want that either. Lungs tight on account of their quarrel and most particularly his response, Athena returned her attention to her meal, ever conscious of Darlington impatiently waiting for her to be done. She took her last bite and followed it with the remainder of her wine. The moment she did so he called for the butler to have her horse readied.

Rising, Athena pushed back her shoulders and told herself she'd done what she could. She'd tried to make up for her wrongdoing – had attempted to convey her sincere regrets and had even offered to make amends. It wasn't her fault if the marquess refused to accept any of it.

Back straight, she exited the dining room with dignity and went to collect her outerwear garments from the foyer. Footsteps followed her every move and when she glanced back, Darlington was there, his expression as stony as ever.

"Where are you staying?" he asked while the butler helped her don her cloak.

"At Foxborough Hall." She hooked the closure at the neck and began putting on her gloves.

Stepping past her, Darlington opened the front door. Annoyance flared inside Athena. She'd not even finished readying herself and already he was showing her the way out.

But rather than wait for her to step over the threshold, he turned to his butler. "Send a message to the stables, Dartwood. Have the grooms ready my horse as well so I may accompany Miss Townsbridge."

Athena spun toward Darlington. "That's really not necessary."

"The weather is getting worse. It would be wrong not to see you back safely."

"I'm sure you would rather stay here."

"What I want became inconsequential the moment you decided to come here." He grabbed his greatcoat with angry movements and shoved his arms through the sleeves. "Now, if you would be so kind, let us not linger any longer."

ATHENA – MISS TOWNSBRIDGE – parted her lips as if prepared to protest, upon which Robert served her the most withering stare he could manage. She promptly snapped her mouth shut and brushed past him, stepping into the chilly outdoors with a frosty mien to match her high temper.

Robert took a fortifying breath and prayed he'd survive the upcoming ride, because the truth was, there was something entirely too enticing about the spirited woman Athena had become. And the fire that burned in her eyes when she spoke – the passion behind her convictions – had seared him to the bone.

Muttering a curse, he followed her out into the cold. He could not – *would* not – allow himself to wonder what she might feel like in his arms, if her lips would part beneath his own in welcome surrender, or if she'd kiss him back with fervor. It was wrong to have such musings. She was his former friend's baby sister for crying out loud. Except she was all woman now, and damn if his body wasn't responding with uncomfortable awareness.

The safest way forward was to keep distance. Stay angry. Show her no mercy. Allow for no closeness. Get her back to Foxborough Hall posthaste. And leave.

Their horses arrived and Robert immediately frowned. "No sidesaddle?"

"I prefer to ride astride," she said.

She'd done so as a child, but as an adult? It seemed outrageous. But the concept was nothing compared with what happened next. With swift movements Athena hefted the front of her skirt and cloak all the way to her waist and raised one booted foot.

Robert stared as she placed it in the stirrup; her entire leg, clad in snug buckskin leather, was put on daring display. His fingers twitched and his muscles flexed. She swung herself into the saddle. He forced his feet into motion. Bloody hell. He'd never be able to get that image out of his head. The shape of her thigh and the curve of her bottom would be imprinted upon his brain forever. He shook his head and mounted his horse while heavy flakes fell with increasing speed.

"Ready?"

Athena gave a curt nod and then they were off, racing through the gates and out onto the country road. A gust of wind swept toward them, tossing snow in their faces.

"I came over the hills to the right," Athena yelled.

It was the quickest route. Robert nodded and steered his horse off the road and across the field. He glanced at his companion to make sure she was all right. Of course she was, he thought wryly. This was Athena Townsbridge, not some delicate flower who couldn't withstand a bit of harsh weather. An odd bit of satisfaction bloomed in his chest. In spite of everything, she was a woman to be admired. Her courage, however destructive it might be on occasion, knew no equal. She'd stood up in church and risked her own reputation to see her brother happy, she'd sought him out at his home when she must have known she'd not be welcome, had risked her reputation again for the sake of making amends, and had voiced her regrets in spite of his censure.

No doubt Athena Townsbridge had more grit than most fully grown men. He did not doubt she'd call out anyone who dared insult those she loved. She'd fight them to the death, because that was the sort of person she was. He knew this – had always known this. She was a force to be reckoned with, and he needed her out of his life right away before he began getting stupid ideas.

"We'll cross the river over there," he shouted, his voice weakened by the increasing wind. Turning slightly in his saddle, he made sure she was still with him. She leaned forward and urged her mount into a faster pace, passing Robert as she raced toward the spot he'd suggested.

With a shake of his head, he followed, only to watch with helpless horror one moment later as her horse reared on its hind legs and threw Athena from the saddle.

Robert reined in his own mount, leapt to the ground, and grabbed the harness. He whistled for Athena's horse as he hurried toward her, pulse leaping with frantic movements at the sight of her looking so still, but the beast was gone.

"Athena." With a groan, she pushed herself into a sitting position, and Robert expelled an immediate breath out of pure relief. *Thank God.* "Are you all right? No. Wait. Don't get up."

"My thigh hurts like the devil, but I think I'll survive."

He crouched beside her. "No sprained ankles then or broken limbs?"

"I don't believe so."

"You're not sure?" His concern for her increased tenfold. "Can you feel your legs?"

She nodded. "Yes."

"And the rest?"

"My bottom is getting a bit cold from sitting here," she confessed. "I'll probably have an ugly bruise tomorrow, but other than that, I'm fine."

He blew out a breath and offered his hand. When she clasped it, he helped her up slowly, then took a moment to assess their surroundings and saw that their path was blocked by branches. "The low visibility masked this fallen tree. If I'd been ahead of you I would most likely have been the one thrown."

"Can we go around it?"

"Yes, but I'm not sure we should." The wind was howling, sweeping snow up off the ground to mix with the flakes that were falling. White mingled with white, obliterating all recognizable landmarks. Thankfully, they were still on his land – an area he could navigate with his eyes closed. "I think we ought to turn back."

"What?"

"Most of our ride still lies ahead. Proceeding in this weather would not only be unwise but extremely foolhardy."

"But I cannot return to your home with you. I mean, coming for a brief visit when no one would be the wiser was one thing. Remaining there until this storm passes is something else entirely. Lord Darlington, I cannot possibly do so."

"I'm sorry, but your safety must come first."

"My family will be beside themselves with worry."

"Perhaps you should have considered that before you set out to visit a bachelor on your own." He hadn't meant to snap at her but lord help him if he wasn't losing whatever remained of his patience. Regretting the outburst, he forced himself to calmly ask, "Does no one know where you were headed?"

"I did inform my lady's maid."

"Well then. There you are. She will no doubt reveal your secret in order to appease your family. They will then realize what happened – that you were forced to seek shelter with me until it was safe to return."

"They might make us marry."

Robert gave her a weary nod. There was no getting around that potential dilemma. "Come. I suggest we return to the warmth of my home before we turn into snowmen. We can continue this discussion there."

He helped her mount his horse, then swung up behind her and gently urged the stallion forward at a moderate pace. Snug between his thighs and with her back pressed into his chest, Robert could not regret what had happened no matter how much he told himself to. He should not find her attractive, nor should he harbor a secret pleasure over the thought of keeping her trapped with him for a while longer. He ought to hate her, despise her, wish her to perdition.

He'd tried that, but it hadn't worked and now, with the weather seemingly wishing to thwart his attempts at adding distance, he might as well surrender himself to the idea of having her near. A lot could happen while she remained in his care. A spike of arousal swept through him in spite of the cold. It had been months since he'd last been this close to a woman. Cursing himself for the scoundrel he was, he tightened his grip on the reins.

"Please ready a room for Miss Townsbridge," he told Dartwood when they returned. "The weather seems to be against us, so she shall be staying here. For the moment."

"Yes, my lord," Dartwood said without displaying the slightest hint of shock. "Shall I have a couple of hot baths prepared?"

"Please do," Robert said. He helped Athena off with her cloak. It did not escape his notice that she was trembling. He met Dartwood's gaze. "Make haste, if you would."

As soon as the butler was gone, Robert tore off his greatcoat and reached for Athena's hands.

"Wha-what are you doing?"

"Helping." He tugged at her gloves, tossed them aside on the hallway table, and brought her hands close to his mouth so he could blow warmth upon them. He rubbed the icy fingers with his own, blew on them once again, and finally, when he was satisfied that the majority of her chill had subsided, pulled her into the parlor so she could warm herself near the fire while they waited.

"I'm such an idiot," he heard her say after a few moments of silence. "Forgive me."

He crossed to the side table and poured two measures of brandy. He handed one of the tumblers to her. "This will soothe your insides and make you feel better."

She took the glass with thanks and drank like a woman who wasn't a stranger to hard spirits. He almost chuckled. Of course she wasn't. She'd probably pilfered her father's liquor before the age of fourteen, if only for the sake of broadening her horizons.

A satisfied sigh left her before she said, "It was wrong of me to come here as I did, to barge in on your life without invitation. I'm sorry. I have an unfortunate inclination to act before I think."

"You don't say."

"And once again with dire consequences for you." She gave her head a violent shake and turned her gaze toward the flickering flames in the grate.

"Let's weather one storm at a time, shall we. As long as we're able to keep your sojourn here a secret, we might get through it without any matrimonial vows at the end." He studied her shapely figure, unable to tear his gaze away – completely unwilling to try. Her gown was made for winter, woolen, with long sleeves and a neckline intended to offer additional warmth. It was proper, save for the contours it put on prominent display.

With her back turned toward him, he feasted his gaze on the base of her neck instead, on the creamy expanse of unblemished skin caught between her upswept hair and the spot where her gown began. The fire crackled and he drew a ragged breath at the thought of trailing his finger along that soft flesh – of pressing a kiss there.

"One can only hope." She turned, her eyes fractured with shards of emotion. "Lord knows I am not the sort of woman any man wants for a wife."

Anger coiled its way around him. He wanted to shout at her, demand she explain why she thought this way, and insist she take the words back. No matter the wrongdoings of her youth, she still deserved to find happiness with a husband who loved her for who she was. No matter how much he'd blamed her over the years, he'd never wished her ill, and he'd certainly never imagined her actions might cause her to think she would be denied an affectionate husband. A thousand words crammed together in his throat, but he could not get a single one out. So he simply stood there, a silent witness to her self-deprecation, until Dartwood came to inform them that their baths had been prepared.

Gritting his teeth, Robert escorted Athena upstairs and directed her toward the bedchamber where she'd be staying. "Meet me in the library when you are ready. There's a great deal more we need to discuss."

Chapter Three

SINKING INTO THE HOT water, Athena savored the bliss of complete relaxation. It had been an eventful day so far and it wasn't over yet. Snatching up the nearby soap, she proceeded to wash herself. The scent of roses mingled with the steam as she worked the soap into a frothy lather. Warmth infused her limbs to chase away any lingering chill. She was safe now, out of the storm.

A helpless smile caught the edge of her mouth. Despite her best efforts to avoid getting into trouble, the weather had chosen to thwart her, landing her under the roof of a man who wanted nothing to do with her. Very well, *best efforts* would in all likelihood have involved not coming here in the first place, but still. Her plan had been perfect to her mind; come, say her piece, and leave.

Setting the soap aside, she sank deeper into the water. She hoped Darlington was right and her maid would tell her family where she had gone so they wouldn't worry too much. Athena's smile slipped. Her parents would have her hide when she returned. And she could not blame them. Once again her reckless behavior – her foolish belief she could fix things with nary a thought to the consequences – threatened to wreak havoc on someone else's life. On Darlington's life.

God. If ever there was a man with the right to despise her, it was he.

She rose from the bath and snatched up a towel. Time to get ready and face the reprimand he would surely give her. When they'd parted ways half an hour earlier, he had not looked the least bit pleased. A sigh left her as she reached for the dress she'd been lent by one of the maids. Her own gown was sopping wet and the hem was covered in flecks of dirt from the ride over, so the housekeeper had insisted on having it cleaned. Although her breeches were fine, she couldn't very well wear them without a shirt.

Choosing not to add her attire to the list of concerns, she rang for a maid to help tie her stays, then put on the dress. Cut from a practical brown shade of cotton, it wasn't as warm as her own, but at least it was dry.

"Would you like me to pin up your hair, miss?" the maid asked.

Athena shook her head. "No thank you. It will dry faster if it's left down."

"Very well, miss."

Athena pushed her feet into the slippers she'd been given and shrugged her shoulders. They were a size too large but they'd have to do while her boots were being dried

Satisfied with her ensemble, she left her room and went downstairs. She recalled where the parlor, study, and dining room were from earlier, so then perhaps this door led to the library? Opening it, she noticed the bookshelves lining the walls and stepped inside. A cozy atmosphere born from the glow of oil lamps, the crackle of burning wood, and the rich smell of leather greeted her.

Searching the space, Athena's gaze landed upon the two armchairs facing the fireplace. One, she noted, was occupied. Her stomach instantly tightened. She tried to force her heart into a calmer rhythm, but to no avail. Darlington's presence affected her in the most peculiar way, instilling in her a curious mixture of apprehension and excitement.

She chastised herself for her silliness and closed the door.

"Miss Townsbridge." Darlington rose and straightened to his full height. An awkward moment of silence followed, during which Athena became extremely aware of her appearance. Her arms were bare, her hair a curly mess around her shoulders, the gown she wore a size too small, and he was staring. Honestly, what must he think of her? He cleared his throat and gestured toward the chair beside his own. "Please, come join me."

Inhaling deeply, she moved toward him with uneven steps as she struggled to keep the oversized slippers on her feet.

"Tea?" Darlington asked once she'd taken her seat and he'd resumed his. Athena nodded and moved to pour herself a cup, only he was swifter. "Allow me."

She sat back, a bit startled by the firm insistence of his voice and by the fact that he, a man, had chosen to fulfill a task ordinarily reserved for women. It was strangely endearing – intimate, even. She shook away the fanciful notion and settled in to watch him serve her.

"Sugar or milk?" he asked, his blue eyes meeting hers as he angled his head in her direction.

"Neither."

A dimple formed at the edge of his mouth as if a smile threatened. The teacup and matching saucer looked tiny between his hands when he picked them up and offered them to her. Athena's stomach tightened further, her fingertips brushing his causing her pulse to leap in the most impractical way.

"Thank you, my lord."

He hovered near her for an additional second before withdrawing to his own chair. When he spoke again, his voice was gruff. "You're welcome."

Athena sipped her tea, allowing the drink to calm her nerves. If only she could escape his company; however, he'd asked her to meet him and as he was her host, she could not deny him. But really, the disquiet she felt in his presence was most unwelcome. And rather than dissipate, it was increasing. Which made no logical sense whatsoever. She'd not been the least bit nervous when she arrived, and yet somehow, with each additional moment spent in his company, she felt herself more unsteady than ever before.

Needing to fill the air with something besides tense silence, she glanced at the book he'd set aside when she'd arrived and asked, "What are you reading?"

"*Ivanhoe.*"

"Really?" Athena turned in her seat so she could better face him. "I adore that story."

Darlington chuckled. "I'm not surprised."

"No?"

"You always were the adventurous sort." He met her gaze and rather than finding censure there, she saw interest. "Remember when you climbed the tree to access the roof on the stables?"

She grinned. "You and my brother were chasing me."

"We were pretending to be officers on a mission to catch a traitor. But you knew Charles was scared of heights and wouldn't come after you. And you were too fast for me. By the time I clambered up onto the roof, you were gone."

"I wasn't far away, though," she said as the memories came flooding back. "I'd slipped through the ventilation hatch and was hiding right beneath you."

"But I looked," he said, his voice incredulous.

"And you probably saw a pile of hay." When he nodded, she smiled. "I was inside it."

"Really?"

She sipped her tea. "If you'd jumped down I'll wager you would have landed on top of me."

Amusement lit his eyes for a moment before they dimmed. A frown appeared on his brow. "I'm sorry for the way I behaved toward you earlier today. Your intentions were good and I...I was unpardonably rude."

"No one would fault you for not desiring to meet with me. Considering the damage I caused you, I certainly cannot. Nor am I able to blame you for not accepting my apology."

"I do, though."

"What?" Her heart gave a hard thud.

"I forgive you, Athena. In fact, I did so a long time ago. After all, you were only a child intent on doing the right thing. It is just that your coming here unannounced caught me completely off guard. I wasn't prepared to face you."

"I'm sorry. I probably should have sent a note."

He answered with a snort. "You've never adhered to protocol, so it's not surprising you did not think to do so."

"I'm sorry."

"So you've said. Multiple times. I wish you would stop." She scrunched her mouth in protest, prompting him to laugh. "Life must be an unbearable struggle for you, having to follow rules, being forced to adhere to social etiquette without compromising your own true self."

He had her pegged to perfection. Athena sank back against her chair with a sigh. "I'm a burden to everyone close to me – a constant threat to everyone's reputation. It's why I'll probably never marry. Because no respectable man will want to take me on. I'm too big a risk."

"You have gumption, Athena. Life with you would never be dull. Indeed, I imagine it would be riveting." His voice was low and strained in a way that surprised her. "You'll find the right man eventually, I'm sure."

"Time will tell, I suppose." She appreciated his attempt to lift her spirit, but she wasn't sure she believed him. Deciding to change the subject before he began suspecting she might want his pity, she asked, "Why have you not married?"

He raised one eyebrow at her. When she did not blink, he eventually said, "After being thrown over twice, I must confess I have not been especially eager to risk a third humiliation."

"Twice?" Athena asked.

"Bethany wasn't my first fiancée. I was engaged to Miss Charlotte Walker a few years prior."

Sweet heavens. Athena didn't know what to say. She felt even worse now, knowing she'd ruined his second attempt to marry.

"I was young and believed Charlotte to be the love of my life. As it turned out, she was only in love with my title. When she realized there wasn't a vast fortune to go along with it, she ran off with my cousin."

The air left Athena's lungs. "No."

"Not that he was wealthy or titled, mind you. Billings was a rake but she was apparently drawn to that."

"Goodness. I'm so—"

"Don't you dare say you're sorry," he told her sternly. "I won't have it."

"Very well then, but I cannot pretend to be glad. I hope Charlotte Walker will regret the choice she made for the rest of her life."

His lips quirked. "I believe she might. As for me, I imagine I was saved from a loveless marriage. Twice, thanks to you."

"If love was what you wanted, then why insist on marrying Bethany?"

"Because I decided to make a practical decision for a change – to choose my wife sensibly instead of using my heart. After all, the heart thing proved a complete disaster so..." He puffed out a breath. "During the last few years I've been busy, working to get my finances in order. Bethany's dowry was supposed to help improve the running of my estate. Without it, I faced a greater challenge, and when my father passed last year, I inherited an unexpected amount of debt."

"Have you managed to pay it off yet?"

"Mostly. I sold the properties that weren't entailed and auctioned off the art he'd collected over the years. With my own investments beginning to show returns, things are finally starting to look up."

Athena nodded. "I'm pleased. You deserve a bit of good fortune after all you've been through."

"Thank you. I appreciate your saying so."

"And if there is anything I can do to help you in some way..." She bit her lip. "Please reconsider the offer I made to you earlier. With my family's help your reputation can be restored."

"I'll consider it, although the very idea of returning to the marriage mart makes me shudder."

She grinned. "I know how you feel."

He watched her pensively for a moment. "Perhaps you've a point, though. If we can show the *ton* we've made amends by stepping out together, there might be hope for us both."

"You think being seen in your company could help my reputation as well?"

"I don't see why not." A thoughtful gleam lit his eyes. "I mean, if I show the world I've forgiven you for what happened, no one else should have cause to blame you. And by dancing with you—"

"Dancing?" she squeaked, her insides shivering at the idea of him holding her close.

"Mm...hmm..." Something dark and dangerous swirled in the depth of his gaze. "I am a marquess, after all. My showing you favor would surely be to your advantage."

"I, um..." Her words caught in her throat. She could not speak or think or even move. All she could do was sit there while he held her captive with the intensity of his stare. Heat washed her skin while tiny sparks danced their way through her. The air grew strained – thick with an odd new awareness she'd never experienced before. She was alone, not with the boy she'd once known, but with the man he'd become, and for the first time in her life, she was scared – scared of the way he made her feel, scared of the power he seemed to wield, scared of what

SOPHIE BARNES

might happen if she gave into the fierce temptation assailing her at this very moment – the reckless desire to climb into his lap and kiss him senseless.

She stood – bolted out of her seat, more like – and crossed to the bookcase furthest away from where he sat. Good heavens. She stared at the shelves and at the vast variety of leather bound volumes they housed. Her hand reached out for support. He'd muddled her head and rendered her breathless. How was that possible?

"Athena?" His voice was too close. She spun around and there he stood, too tall and imposing for her to think straight. He frowned. "Is something the matter?"

She shook her head. "No. Not at all."

"It was just a suggestion," he said. "If you do not wish to dance with me, you obviously shan't have to."

Swallowing, she skirted along the bookcase, removing herself from his vicinity. "All right."

"All right?" He watched her with a puzzled expression, clearly unsure of what she might be agreeing to.

Athena couldn't blame him since she'd no idea herself. She just knew she felt like her world was tilting, and she was falling and somehow he'd made that happen, though she'd no idea how. "I need some more tea."

"Of course."

She gave a curt nod to cement the notion, to cement herself, and went to collect her cup.

ROBERT WATCHED ATHENA walk away. Flee, more like, to the safety of her chair. His chest tightened. The suggestion they dance together had clearly alarmed her. He clenched his fists and tried not to feel too affronted. Instead, he forced himself to think clearly – rationally – without emotion fogging his brain. Athena was brave. She never ran from anything. Why, then, would she run from him?

He pondered his own response to her – the inappropriate attraction he could not deny. Lord help him, he'd not thought she could look more tempting than when she'd put her entire leg on display while mounting her horse, but he'd been wrong. The dress she presently wore, while modest and drab in cut and color, fit her so snugly he could not ignore her luscious curves. Christ, how he longed to slide his palm over her, to cup and squeeze her until she begged for more.

He was a cad. A disgusting bastard who needed to get his head out of the gutter.

But what if...

What if the attraction was not one sided? What if she experienced it too?

He knit his brow.

Could it be possible?

It was the only thing he could think of that might distress her. Especially if she did not understand what was happening. Equally thrilled and appalled by the prospect of him appealing to her on a more elemental level, he forced himself to remain where he was, to turn his back and quietly study his bookshelf while giving himself time to think and her a chance to regain her composure.

His heart knocked hard against his ribs. They'd only just been reunited. She was a Townsbridge. He could not allow himself to act rashly. Removing himself to a nearby window, he gave his attention to the outdoors, only to find himself gazing at her reflection in the glass. He had to marry one day. His last two attempts had led to disaster. Finding a woman who'd want him after the ordeal he'd been through would be a chore. And Athena owed him.

No. That wouldn't do.

He could not permit himself to pursue her unless he did so for the right reasons.

His muscles responded, tightening at the idea of having her all to himself. There was certainly one reason he could think of. Their marriage would not lack passion. And she needed someone firm to guide her – to reel her in and keep her safe.

A smirk caught his lips. He glanced at where she sat. Firelight played upon her skin and with her mass of curly brown hair flowing over her shoulders, she looked divine. Lowering his gaze to the swell of her bosom, he dug his fingertips into his palms and clenched his jaw. Yes. He wanted her. More than he'd wanted Charlotte, more than he'd wanted Bethany, more than he'd ever wanted anything else in the world. He wanted to possess Athena's fiery spirit, to bask in the pleasure he knew he'd find in her arms, to savor the joy she would bring to his life, the vitality of her nature. She was what he required – the path to true happiness. Perhaps even to love. And how the hell he'd not seen that years before was beyond him.

Because she'd been a child.

That was no longer the case. Thank Christ.

Nervous trepidation skipped through him. It had been years since he'd romanced anyone. He scarcely knew where to begin.

Slowly, his instinct warned, *and by ensuring she might be open to his advances.*

After all, the very last thing he desired was a repeat rejection. Coming from her, he doubted he'd ever recover. He took a steady breath, tried to find some sense of calm. Nothing else had ever counted as much as his next words would.

"Do you still collect flowers?" He'd not really known what he'd say until he'd said it, and somehow the question seemed perfect. The subject was safe, allowing them, he hoped, to return to a more relaxed mood.

She turned slightly in her chair so she could watch his approach. "Yes. I'm surprised you remember."

He studied her as he drew nearer, noted how she averted her gaze and started to fidget. Forcing a casual lilt to his voice, he said, "How could I not? You were always searching for four leaf clovers and marveling over plants you'd never seen before."

A grin brightened her features. "I have ten notebooks now, filled with my flowers and notes."

"Ten? That's rather impressive."

"No replicas," she added. "Each flower is unique."

"I'm guessing some must have come from a hothouse."

"A few, I'll confess." She tilted her head and gave him a smile. "Do you still dabble in poetry?"

"Poetry? I don't recall ever—"

"The barmaid down yonder, does make one wonder, about gravitational forces. Her breasts are so large, they're in need of a barge, while her arse needs a team of ten horses."

Robert barely managed to wait for her to finish before a roar of laughter rolled through him. "Good God. You remember that?"

"Of course. Bawdy rhymes have a way of sticking with me, Lord Darlington."

Interesting.

He considered asking if she'd invented any of her own. Instead he said, "I know I insisted on formal address earlier, but I think we can dispense with that now. Please, call me Robert."

"If you like."

The hesitance in her voice did not escape his notice. Deciding to set her at ease, he prepared to return to the amusing subject they'd been discussing, but was stopped from doing so when Dartwood came to announce that supper was ready to be served.

Thanking the butler, Robert waited for Athena to rise and then offered his arm. She stared at him for a moment as if unsure of how to proceed. When he did not budge, she eventually looped her hand through the crook of his elbow and let him escort her. Satisfaction settled deep within his chest. He dropped a look at the lady who walked by his side and was pleased to see a pink flush in her cheeks.

Yes, he affected her. And he rather imagined it terrified her to bits.

Chapter Four

WHEN ATHENA HAD WOKEN the next day from a dream involving Robert's embrace, she'd known she had to clear her head, and in order to do so she needed to busy herself with something. What she hadn't needed was to sit still and think. Doing so would only make matters worse.

Putting her arm muscles into the task at hand, she slid the shovel's blade under the straw, lifted, and carried. The snow had not let up during the night. Getting to the stables had been an ordeal in and of itself.

Tossing the dirty hay in the muck pile, she went back inside to continue her work – a necessary reprieve from the constant reminder of what had occurred the previous day, and from the man who'd lodged himself in her mind. Lord help her, she could not stop thinking of him or of the mad sensations he stirred in her.

Surely, this wasn't normal behavior.

She snorted and filled her shovel once more. Of course it wasn't. This was her, for heaven's sake, and nothing about her had ever been normal. Shaking her head, she muttered a curse and continued cleaning until the stall floor was bare. After stretching her back and rolling her shoulders, she went to collect some fresh straw.

"Allow me to help," one of the grooms said.

"No thank you. I can easily manage." She hefted a bale up into her arms and staggered along with it, certain she heard him say something pertaining to stubborn females. Athena ignored him and kept going. When she reached the stall she dropped the bale inside and panted for breath. It truly was heavy, but it gave her the exercise she required.

She grabbed a knife and cut the twine that bound the straw together, then used a pitchfork to loosen it up so it could be scattered across the ground. Once this had been done, she grabbed another bale and hauled it to the stall. Bending at the waist, she began cutting the twine as she'd done on the previous one and was just about to straighten when a rough voice spoke from directly behind her.

"What the hell are you doing?"

Jolted by Robert's unexpected presence, Athena sucked in a breath and turned to find him scowling at her. It didn't help that he looked every bit as handsome as he'd done the day before. She'd rather hoped he wouldn't – that the attraction she'd experienced had been the product of her imagination and that the dream she'd had would seem ridiculous when she saw him again.

It did not.

If anything, his glower had the strangest effect. Her stomach fluttered while heat slid through her veins. "I'm mucking out the stalls and giving the horses fresh hay."

His gaze slid over her—over the snug woolen jacket she wore and down the length of her breeches. To her astonishment, his expression hardened further. "You'll catch your death out here."

"The exercise keeps me warm."

He knit his brow. "I won't have you working like some common laborer."

"But I—"

"You're a guest here, Athena. Please try to behave as one."

The comment smarted. "I don't like sitting about doing nothing."

"Then I shall have to find a task for you indoors. One that does not involve you parading about in front of my grooms like that."

He fairly hissed the last part. Athena scrunched her nose and gave herself a swift once over. "Like what?"

He pinched the bridge of his nose and swore before leveling her with his gaze once more. "You're not a little girl anymore."

"I know I'm not."

"Do you?" he growled.

Unnerved by his strange possessive behavior, she took a step back. "I've work to do. I'll see you inside the house once I'm done."

"The devil you will."

Without another word he grabbed her around her waist, hefted her up and over his shoulder, and started walking.

Athena squealed. "Put me down this instant."

"No."

"I'm warning you, Robert. I'll scream."

"Go right ahead."

She cursed him to perdition instead.

"Where did you get the jacket?" he asked once he'd brought her into his study and set her back on her feet.

Raising her chin, Athena crossed her arms and gave him her best glare. "I borrowed it from one of your footmen."

"Of all the..." He spun away and scrubbed his hand across his face. A curse followed and then he faced her once again. "You'll need to return it. Immediately."

"Did you think I was planning on keeping it?"

"No, I..." He huffed a breath and before she knew what was happening, he was holding her by her upper arms and leaning in. Stormy eyes locked onto hers. "There's brazen, and then there's plain foolhardiness. You cannot honestly think you can walk around dressed like that without anyone taking notice?"

Athena blinked. "I don't see how my choice in clothes is any business of yours. You're not my father or my brother."

"No, I'm most certainly not," he told her with a fierceness that took her aback. "But that doesn't mean you are not my responsibility while you are here or that I shouldn't be honest with you. The fact is, you are providing every man who sees you like this with a fantasy that will stir his loins for the rest of his days."

Shock thundered through her. His words and what they implied were beyond the pale. No one had ever spoken to her with such crassness before. She clenched her jaw and glared back at him. "How dare you?"

"It's time for you to be made aware," he told her darkly. "You no longer have a child's body. In case you hadn't noticed."

She turned her gaze away from his and stared at the wall behind him while taking deep breaths. "I cannot very well muck out a stall while wearing a dress. That wouldn't be practical."

"Perhaps you ought to leave the mucking out of stalls to the grooms then?"

She huffed in response to that and crossed her arms in protest. "Fine."

He released his hold and took a step back. "Athena, I'm not telling you this to be difficult. If I didn't care about you or your wellbeing, I'd let you gad about as you please."

Acceptance wasn't easy, but the sincerity in his voice cut through her defenses until she was forced to acknowledge his point. "I know I can be a handful and that I am not the easiest person to deal with."

"There's nothing wrong with being feisty," he told her gently. "In fact, I marvel at your vivacity. But your innocent naïveté puts you in danger."

"I'm not as naïve as you think," she grumbled. "I know there are villains about in the world. My sister-in-law, James' wife, Abigail, almost became the victim of one."

"And yet you still ride around the countryside unchaperoned, intent on visiting a man who for all you knew could have harbored ill intentions toward you. What if I'd been plotting a chance for revenge?"

"Were you?"

"That's not the point and you know it."

"I never go anywhere unarmed," she tried, hoping to offer him some reassurance.

He stared at her, then slowly nodded. "All right. Show me your weapon."

Reaching down, Athena pulled a knife loose from her boot and held it up for his inspection. Pleasure burst through her when she saw the approving look in his eyes. Good. Now he'd know she wasn't as careless about her safety as he'd assumed. She raised her chin and met his gaze boldly.

"Stay right there. Don't move." He crossed to the door several paces away, then turned back to face her. "Now, pretend I'm a murderous scoundrel determined to have my way with you before I slit your throat. Defend yourself."

"What?" The word was barely out before he was upon her, one hand grabbing her wrist so roughly she let go the knife. Athena narrowed her gaze at the slate blue eyes staring back at her. "That's not fair. I wasn't ready."

"We'll do it again then." Releasing her, he returned to his previous position and started advancing once more.

This time, Athena managed to dodge him once before he caught her wrist and pushed her back against the wall, trapping her there, his hand adding pressure until she was forced to release the knife once more.

She frowned at him. "I don't want to hurt you. Obviously, if you were a real attacker I would have stabbed you."

With a snort of clear disbelief, he let her go and went back to the door. "Do it. Try to stab me, Athena."

"I can't."

He tilted his head as if in thought, then went to his desk and opened a drawer. "Use this instead of your knife, then."

Accepting the wooden ruler he held toward her, she returned the knife to her boot. With the ruler clasped in her hand, she took a deep breath and readied herself for his next attack. When it came, she swung her arm. The ruler grazed his shoulder before he managed to grab her wrist once more. Instinct brought her knee up, but rather than connecting with him her legs swung out to the side, meeting air right before she landed on her back. Straddling her, Robert pinned her arms above her head, removed the ruler from her grasp with unsettling ease, and tossed it aside.

"Do you believe me now?"

Athena stared up at Robert. She'd never felt more vulnerable before, nor had she ever been as aware of another person. Ragged breaths squeezed her lungs in accordance with her jittery heartbeats. He was leaning over her, holding her captive, his face so close she was able to see the small imperfections marring his skin— a tiny scar on his chin, a small bump almost hidden against the side of his nose. His eyes gleamed with smug satisfaction, but it was his smell that stirred her awareness the most. Earthy, with hints of morning coffee, it instilled in her a desire so fierce she believed she might die if he did not kiss her.

"Yes."

One word – a whisper stirring the air with possibility.

His grip on her tightened. Her breaths grew increasingly ragged.

"Athena." He murmured her name. His nostrils flared and she saw his lips part. The blue in his eyes deepened.

"Yes," she whispered again.

He swallowed, his throat working as if in accordance with some impossible chore. And then, as swiftly as he'd knocked her off her feet, he pulled her upright and stepped away. "Get changed so we can have breakfast. Once we've eaten, I'll teach you how to defend yourself properly."

A queer sense of disappointment raced through her. She studied him as he stood there, partly turned away from her. Incomprehension snapped at her from every angle. She didn't understand what was going on, why she was being assaulted by all these perplexing sensations. He'd had her in a position that ought to have terrified her, and yet, against all odds, it had thrilled her. She'd wanted him to kiss her, for heaven's sake. Nothing about what had happened between them just now made an ounce of sense. A burn of humiliation heated her cheeks as she spun away and went to the door, fleeing from him and from the power he wielded over her.

CLOSING HIS EYES, ROBERT waited until he heard her climbing the stairs before he dared move. Christ, he was a fool. What the hell had he been thinking, putting her on the floor like that with himself on top? The position had been indecent – too close a resemblance to that of lovemaking. And she'd responded. By God, he could still envision her parted lips, the sigh with which she told him, "yes," the glazed look of passion brightening her eyes as he'd leaned in.

When he'd learned she was in the stables, he'd gone to fetch her. Anger had not assailed him until he'd spotted one of the grooms. The lad had been ogling Athena's leather-clad bottom with a leer so base Robert had nearly knocked his block off. Instead, he'd tightened his jaw and jerked the groom aside. The lad had gasped and scampered away, leaving Robert to deal with his hoydenish guest on his own.

But to think he was able to show her the threat she invited without repercussion had provided him with a lesson in ignorance too. Regardless of her efforts to thwart social stricture in pursuit of freedom, Athena was used to a sheltered life. She'd been raised as a lady and it was his duty to treat her as such, not to toss her to the ground and have his way.

"Damn."

He raked his fingers through his hair, took a series of deep inhalations, and waited for the surge of lust he'd experienced moments earlier to subside. Drooling after her and getting himself all wound up with need was not the way to woo her. A swift glance at the window confirmed the snow persisted. He hoped it would soon stop so he could get her back to Foxborough Hall and court her as she deserved. Because, by God, he would make her his. Athena needed a husband with a firm hand – a man who could keep her safe without stifling her spirit – someone who knew her well enough to appreciate her vibrant nature.

Robert took a deep breath and felt his chest tighten. He knew he could be that man. The idea of letting another take on the role was insupportable. He thought of Charlotte and Bethany. Compared to them, Athena shone like a blazing star. Thank God, Charlotte had run off with Billings, and thank God, Bethany had ended up with Charles. If Robert had married either, he would have had to watch Athena grow up and get courted by someone else, and that would in all likelihood have driven him insane.

Heading toward the dining room, he braced himself for what was to come. Facing Charles again would be unavoidable. They'd have to talk and while he did not relish the prospect of doing so, he'd suffer through the ordeal for her because...

He halted. It was too soon to suppose he'd fallen in love with her. Wasn't it? Love took time to manifest. He'd never believed it could strike a person at first sight. Only a superficial appreciation for good looks had the power to do so. As did lust. And yes, he thought Athena stunning. He desired her. But surely that wasn't all that drove him.

With a shake of his head he accepted the truth. They'd been part of each other's lives for what seemed like forever. Even if they'd not seen each other these past six years and even though she'd been but fourteen years of age the last time they'd met, with him engaged to someone else, no less, he *knew* her. More than that, he felt he understood her. He certainly admired her. They had a bond – one that stretched back almost two decades.

Continuing his onward stride, Robert reached the dining room. Letting Athena go was out of the question. He enjoyed her company, her challenging nature, her individuality. Seeing her again had unlocked something deep within him. It was just a matter of time before he lost his heart to her completely. The only question was whether or not she'd return his regard.

Later that afternoon, after a far more appropriate lesson in self-defense during which he'd kept a respectable distance from Athena while teaching her how to block an attack and how to avoid getting overpowered, he made his way to the library. They'd concluded her lesson with luncheon, after which he'd returned to his study to work for a couple of hours while she relaxed with a book. After informing Dartwood that he was to let him know immediately if Athena attempted to go outside, he'd seen to some correspondence, reviewed his ledger, and contemplated the offer he'd make for her when he eventually met with her father.

Reaching the library, he opened the door and prepared to step inside, only to come to an instant halt the moment he saw her. Belly down on the floor and with her feet kicked up in the air, she read one of three books strewn out before her. Every muscle inside Robert flexed in response, for although she was properly dressed now in the same gown she'd worn when she first arrived, her skirt had followed the laws of gravity and lay around her knees, allowing him a direct look at stocking-clad calves and feet.

He frowned. Where the devil were her shoes?

Searching the floor, his gaze swept the curve of her bottom. No breeches this time, his treacherous brain informed him. And her skirts were already bunched half-way up her legs. Robert flexed his fingers. It wouldn't take much to...

With a shake of his head he turned away, slamming the door as he left the room. If he didn't know better, he'd think she meant to torment him. But no. He'd seen the incomprehension in her gaze earlier when she'd been struck by desire. She'd not understood it or known how to handle it. She'd simply lain there, willing to surrender as instinct took over. Which wasn't at all what he wanted from her. What he wanted, he thought as he grabbed his greatcoat and stormed from the house in pursuit of the wintry chill outside, was for her to come to him without fear or doubt but with full understanding of what would transpire between them.

"I missed you this afternoon," she told him at dinner. "You said you would come to the library when you were done with your work, but you didn't. Or was that you, slamming the door?"

"It was. I'm sorry." He continued eating his soup.

"Is everything all right?"

"It is."

"You're not angry with me again?"

"No. I just..." He frowned at her. "Eat, Athena, or your food will get cold."

She made a huffing sound, but did as he asked. Pleased with her compliance, he finished the remainder of his soup in silence and set his spoon aside. "Perhaps we can play a game of chess after dinner. Or cards, if you prefer."

She wrinkled her nose. "I'm not especially good at strategy games. I wonder... Do you still have your marbles?"

Robert instantly grinned. "Of course. They're upstairs in my bedchamber."

"Then I would suggest you fetch them once we've completed our meal so we can compete. As I recall, you won the last time we played and I've a good mind to change that."

Amused and, he had to confess, eager to have some fun with her, as soon as the meal was over, Robert went to collect the box of marbles he kept on top of his dresser. They'd been his most prized possession once – a collection that had taken him years of birthdays, Christmases, and pocket money to establish. Arriving in the parlor where Athena waited, he set the box on the floor and sat down beside it. She came to join him and he poured the marbles out onto the carpet.

"This one was always my favorite," she said, picking up a hand cut agate marble, its high polish making it stand out among the ones made from clay.

"Mine too. It was a gift from my favorite aunt. She'd seen me eye it every time we passed the shop window, so she bought it for me for my birthday. My tenth one, I think."

Athena chuckled. "Just imagine. It's as old as I am."

The comment gave him pause. He glanced at her, at the smile curving her lips, the rosy flush in her cheeks, at how a few stray curls hung over her brow while she studied the rest of his collection. He was ten years her senior. Wanting anything more than friendship from her wasn't right. It just wasn't. And yet, he could not deny his feelings. All he could do was hope and pray he'd be good enough for her and that she would not regret marrying him.

He gave himself an inward shake. There was no guarantee she'd accept his hand, but now was not the time to dwell on such detail. Removing a long piece of red ribbon at the bottom of the box, he laid it out in a circular shape and placed all the marbles inside.

"Pick your shooter. *Not* that one," he said when she reached for the agate marble. "That one stays in the middle, to be won by the most skilled player."

"Oh, all right." She gave him a cheeky smile followed by a low chuckle and selected a yellow clay marble of medium size. Robert picked out a similar one painted blue. "May I begin?"

"By all means." Robert watched as she flicked her marble forward with remarkable speed and accuracy, pushing a green marble out of the ring. Athena scooped up both marbles. He narrowed his gaze on her. "You've been practicing."

"I have a niece and nephew now. They love to play."

"I see." Robert flicked his own marble and was relieved to find he'd not lost his touch as it pushed two others out of the ring so he could collect them.

They continued to play until the only remaining marble in the ring was the one cut from polished agate. Robert had no doubt he would win it. It was his turn after all, and he wasn't about to *let* Athena claim the final prize. She'd had her turn already and missed. Gauging the distance and the speed with which he would have to flick his blue marble, Robert aimed and shot it toward the one made from agate. A gratifying clank sounded as they connected and the blue marble pushed the agate one out of the ring.

"You win," Athena said, not sounding the least bit put out. She'd always been a good sport.

He picked the marble up so it rested between his thumb and index finger, then turned toward her. "Do I?"

Her eyes met his in question. She glanced at the marble, then back at him. A soft laugh left her. "Of course. You cleared the last marble and you also have the highest count."

"Athena." He wasn't sure what the hell he was doing. Allowing instinct to guide him, he supposed. He held the marble toward her. "I want you to have this."

She shook her head. "I couldn't possibly. Robert, it's your most precious one."

"Which is why it would mean a great deal to me if it belonged to you."

Her entire face turned a brilliant shade of red. She shook her head again and then she suddenly stood and backed toward the door. "No. I mean, no thank you."

He'd rushed her. He could see that now. By revealing his intentions before she was ready, he'd pushed her away. Sitting there on the floor, surrounded by scattered marbles, he cursed himself for his stupidity. Taming a woman like Athena took time; winning her would require a great deal of skill.

THE NEXT DAY BROUGHT relief in several shapes and forms. For one thing, the blizzard had stopped and the sun had come out. Athena would be able to leave Darlington House and return to Foxborough Hall – a point she made sure to get across during breakfast. And for another, Robert remained scarce while the servants worked to clear the front steps and driveway. When she did see him, he treated her cordially, without any hint of wanting to give her more than what she'd come for – an end to six years of guilt and the chance to move on.

"We'll set off as soon as we've finished eating," he told her when they met for luncheon. "The snow is fairly deep so I expect the ride to take us twice as long as usual."

She nodded her agreement and added a smile. "Thank you for your hospitality, and for your forgiveness. It means a great deal."

The look he gave her in return was full of warmth. "I am hoping it will allow for a new beginning."

"So you will speak with Charles then and try to make amends with him?"

"I plan to. Yes."

Her smile widened. "Oh, thank you, Robert. I cannot tell you how relieved I am to hear it."

He held her gaze while he sipped his wine, inviting a lovely bit of heat to swirl up inside her. They had, against all odds, become friends during the last two days. She'd pestered him, tried his every last nerve, she was sure, and he'd scolded her for it. But not without a valuable lesson. While her parents and siblings would oftentimes roll their eyes at her behavior, treat her like an impossible child or like an impending threat to their reputations, Robert had tried to tame her without compromising her nature.

She wondered at this and could not refrain from asking, "Do you like me, Robert?"

The question seemed to freeze his movements. He gave her a careful look. "What do you mean, exactly?"

Taking courage, she said, "Most people outside my family try to avoid me. I don't really have any friends and the ones I did have as a child mysteriously disappeared after Charles's wedding. Given my personality, I cannot help but wonder if it was my *faux pas* that turned me into a pariah, or if I'm simply too unruly to like."

"You are aware that most members of the *ton* are idiots, are you not?"

The seriousness with which he posed the question made her laugh. "Maybe."

He pushed out a breath and set his glass aside. "I like you a great deal, Athena."

"Really?"

"To be sure, you do get the strangest notions sometimes, and I do believe you've got a great deal to learn about life and how to manage your willfulness so you don't put yourself or others in danger. But as a person, I think you're a gem. I'd hate to see you lose your sparkle."

Athena's lips parted in response to his words. She wanted to thank him and yet somehow doing so seemed insufficient when he'd just given her the biggest stamp of approval she'd ever received. Coming from him, from the man whose life she'd ruined, it meant the world. It made her eyes sting and her throat close up tight, so rather than speak, she simply nodded her appreciation and finished her food. The prospect of leaving his side instilled in her the strangest feeling of discontent. In fact, she feared she would miss him terribly once they parted ways. More than that, she feared she would lose her opportunity to learn why her heart beat faster when he was near or why his opinion mattered as much as it did. Within her reach was the chance to figure out something important, and yet, she couldn't quite seem to grasp it.

Chapter Five

ROBERT'S GUT TIGHTENED as he and Athena approached Foxborough Hall. He'd never been prone to anxiety, but the thought of walking through the front doors he could see in the distance and coming face to face with Athena's family, of giving explanations and then embarking on the most important endeavor of his life, made his nerves clang together.

"Tell me something," he said. They'd had almost two hours in which to speak, and yet he'd managed to waste them on inane topics and introspection. Walking their horses through deep banks of snow, they turned them onto the tree-lined drive leading up to the house. "What is your hope for the future?"

"To be happy, I suppose."

"And what would happiness entail?"

"I don't know. I'd like to be respected by my peers, not to be gawked at or whispered about whenever I enter a room."

"What about courtship, marriage, and children?"

She cast him a startled look. "I, um..." Turning her gaze back toward the road, she swallowed deeply, then said, "I would like to have a family of my own one day – a large one, I should think, with plenty of children and an adoring husband to love."

Warmth seeped through Robert's veins. "Do you have a particular gentleman in mind yet?"

"No. As I've mentioned, none of the well-respected gentleman I've met wants to risk his reputation on me, but I am hoping that will change if we're seen together. Your public acceptance of me, as the man I once wronged, would help a great deal, I'm sure."

"Let us hope so," he murmured.

So she'd not set her cap for anyone in particular. This was good to know since it increased his chances and eased his mind. All he had to do now was open her eyes to what he already knew to be true – that they could have a passionate union filled with many more joyful moments and interesting conversation. Within the confines of his heart he could feel his own emotions shifting, from the almost brotherly affection he'd harbored for her as a boy, to the fierce adoration and want she instilled in him as a man. It was more than purely physical. It was an innate need to protect her, to walk by her side and offer guidance, to bask in the beauty of her sparkling eyes and bathe in the warmth of her smiles.

A shaky breath rose from his lungs. They had arrived.

After dismounting, Robert went to help Athena down. He knew she didn't require help, but he wanted to give it nonetheless, to take this last bit of closeness for himself. His hands circled her waist and she slid easily into his arms. No words passed between them, but he could see understanding bloom in the depth of her gaze. Her lips parted, but no sound escaped her. Instead, she just gazed at him in bewildered silence.

Robert's hold on her tightened, ever so briefly – just enough to convey there was more between them than friendship on his part – and then he took a step back and turned for the door.

"Robert?"

Her voice, breathy with uncertainty, prompted him to swing back toward her. She was staring at him as if seeing him for the very first time. Apparently, the intimate moments they'd shared these past two days and the manner in which she'd responded to him were beginning to click into place. He smiled, offered a soft nod to tell her she wasn't alone, and proceeded up the front steps.

The door opened on the third knock. A servant – clearly the butler – appeared, but the man barely managed to get a single word out before several women crowded together behind him. One was Athena's mother, Lady Roxley, another was Athena's older sister, Sarah. Then there was Lady Foxborough and a couple of women he did not recognize.

"What's all the fuss?" The voice belonged to Athena's father, Viscount Roxley.

"My lord and lady," Robert said when the butler moved aside. "I have come to return your daughter to your care."

"Darlington?" Lady Roxley gave him a shocked stare before brushing past him so she could embrace her daughter. "Goodness, Athena. We've been ever so worried."

"I'm sorry, Mama. The weather wouldn't permit me to return until now."

"Well." Her mother gave a tight smile. "Let's get you inside. I'm sure you'd appreciate a hot cup of tea while you tell us what happened."

Robert watched her go. The rest of the women followed. Robert met Lord Roxley's gaze. "I am hoping you will permit me to have a moment of your time, my lord."

Roxley gave him a solemn nod. "Of course."

"I shall make sure the horses are cared for until you are ready to leave," the butler said.

Thanking him, Robert entered the house and removed his greatcoat, hat, and gloves. He handed them all to a nearby footman and followed Roxley toward a door to the right. The earl gave the room a swift look before he entered and beckoned for Robert to join him. Robert stepped inside what appeared to be the music room.

"My entire family is here at the moment so finding privacy can be a chore," Roxley explained. "Would you like refreshment?"

"I wouldn't say no to a hot cup of coffee and something to eat. If it's not any trouble."

"Not at all." Roxley rang for a maid and put in the order, then turned to Robert. "Please have a seat."

Robert claimed a spot on a wide sofa upholstered in green and gold-striped silk. Roxley chose the adjacent armchair. "Your daughter came to see me with the best of intentions. She wished to apologize for her part in breaking things off between me and Bethany six years ago – or rather, for the manner in which she went about it."

"I see." Roxley stared straight back at him with unyielding eyes.

Robert steeled himself against the intimidating expression. "When the snow began, we tried to return, but the weather worsened and it became too hazardous for us to proceed." He decided to omit the part about her fall. "So we returned to Darlington House and waited for the blizzard to stop."

"In other words, you and Athena have been living together for the last two days, she without a chaperone and you..." Roxley tilted his head. "Did anything untoward happen between you?"

"No."

Roxley held his gaze for a long moment until the maid bringing coffee and sandwiches served as a welcome interruption. Robert let out a sigh of relief. When the maid was gone, Roxley said, "I always liked you, Darlington. I'm extremely sorry for the manner in which you were treated. Athena's actions were inexcusable."

"I thought so too. At the time."

"Oh?"

Robert poured them each a cup of coffee and added milk to his own. He took a sip, then prepared a plate for himself with a couple of sandwiches. Leaning back, he took a couple of bites before saying, "Bethany is better off with Charles. They love each other, so from that point of view everything is as it should be."

"Nevertheless, your reputation suffered. And that is without considering Charles's betrayal. He was your friend."

"I'm very much aware."

"He hasn't recovered from what he did. The guilt still dogs him."

Only three days earlier, hearing as much would have given Robert great satisfaction. Now, he was simply tired of all the anger. He wanted to move on, start fresh, find happiness for himself. "Perhaps it is time for me to speak with him – to make an attempt at restoring our friendship."

"You would do that?"

"Yes."

Roxley raised his eyebrows and looked at him with pure consternation. "What on earth did Athena say to make you change your mind?"

So Roxley knew his son had made repeated attempts at patching things up over the years. Robert had only responded once – in a manner he wasn't the least bit proud of.

"Nothing, in particular," he said. "But spending time with her reminded me of what I truly lost that day six years ago – the welcoming warmth of this family. I was very fond of my summer visits to your estate in the Lake District, and I find that I've missed it – that I've missed you. All of you."

"Well." Roxley sank back against his seat with a startled breath. "I must say I'm surprised."

"It would mean a great deal to me if you would be willing to join me for supper at my home on Saturday."

"I'm afraid we have the dance at the assembly hall that evening, but Monday ought to work. If that suits you?"

"It does." And now he knew about the dance as well. Perfect. He finished his sandwiches, then said, "I trust no one outside this house will learn of Athena's overnight stay at my home."

"Of course not," Roxley said.

"And you will make no demands of either of us?"

"My intention has always been to offer my children support. Pushing any of them into an unwanted union would only make them miserable."

"Good." He'd been hoping her parents would not force her hand since he wanted to be her choice. Still, he felt compelled to say, "I would have done my duty if you'd asked me to."

"Understood." Roxley cleared his throat. "But no matter how you may feel about Athena, I love my daughter and mean for her to be happy. Besides, I cannot imagine you'd want to get yourself leg-shackled to the woman who broke up your wedding and damaged your reputation."

"As I believe we've already established, opinions do change."

Roxley gave him an uncertain look. "What are you saying?"

Steeling himself, Robert said, "I'd like your permission to court her."

The viscount gaped at him for a full three seconds before laughter shook him. "You must be joking."

"I can assure you I am not."

"But...but..." Roxley waved his hands as if trying to catch the words that escaped him. "You cannot possibly want Athena."

Bristling at the shock in Roxley's voice, Robert said, "Why the hell wouldn't I?"

"Well she's...she's—"

"I suggest you choose your words wisely, Roxley."

Roxley blinked. "She's my daughter and I adore her, but that doesn't mean I don't know she's a handful. And then there's the whole business of your past and... Good God. Is this your way of exacting revenge?"

"That's a bloody insulting question to ask," Robert growled. "Not only because of what you think me capable of but because you clearly can't comprehend what I see in her."

"Well," Roxley said with great hesitation. "What *do* you see in her?"

"A woman with a lively spirit, someone who would challenge my mind while bringing joy to my life, the sort of person with whom I would never be bored but in whose company my view of the world would be improved. Athena is a delight. Feisty and brazen, yes. But I like that about her."

"You do?"

"I cannot imagine why no one else would. She's the red poppy in the field of white daisies, the flame that burns brighter than all the rest. She has energy and a will stronger than any other I've ever encountered."

"A characteristic that tends to get her into trouble."

"Which is why she ought to marry as quickly as possible, so she can get settled. Preferably with a man who will love her for who she is while offering guidance."

"And you wish to be that man?"

"I do," Robert said. "More than anything."

Roxley gave him an odd look. "She matters to you. That much is clear. But how can you possibly guarantee love after only two days in her company?"

Robert wasn't quite sure. He knew he harbored strong feelings for her, but he wasn't yet ready to call it love. He cleared his throat and told her father, "Because I cannot stand the idea of being apart from her for one moment – of having to leave her here and not see her for several days, of not being able to hear her voice and sense her presence, of having to dine without her while wondering what she's up to – if she is getting herself into trouble – of wishing she'd simply be there to favor me with a smile."

His breath caught. Good God. He loved her already. It was the only explanation for how he felt. Not that he understood it one bit. He'd have thought it took longer to develop such deep emotion and yet, perhaps because they had known each other for as long as they had, she'd only had to grow up in order for him to lose his heart to her completely.

Baffled, Robert gave his head a shake.

Roxley drank some coffee and set his cup aside. "I must confess I'm shocked. But I suppose if your intentions are as pure as you profess, it could work. As long as she is willing."

When the viscount raised one eyebrow in question, Robert said, "I think she could be, in time. As it is right now, I'm not sure she knows how she feels about me."

"I see. So what you're requesting is a chance to meet with her – to further your acquaintance with her, so to speak, in the hope that she might come around to your way of thinking?"

"Exactly."

"Hmm... I'll need to know the state of your finances, Darlington. Not that I would let money or the lack thereof stand in the way of a happy union. We'd find a way around that if necessary. But I hate surprises, and I would like to make sure you're not simply after her dowry."

Every muscle inside Robert clamped tight like a vice. He clenched his fists, but there was no getting around this. "My father left a substantial debt. I've managed to clear most of it over the course of the last year."

"By selling off property and art?"

"You've been following my activities, I see."

Roxley snorted. "It was in the papers."

"My own personal income has taken time to secure. It's not as large as I'm hoping it will be in a couple of years from now, but it is enough to provide a comfortable life for Athena without touching her dowry."

"How much are we talking, exactly?"

"Two thousand pounds per annum."

"Not an impressive sum, I'll grant you that, but not a terrible one either. Returns on an investment?"

"Indeed. I bought shares in a couple of businesses based in New York. They were small when I met with the owners on that trip where Bethany and I were introduced, but have since begun to grow. Apparently, there's a future in agriculture and steel."

"You don't say," Roxley mused.

"I'd be happy to show you the pertinent papers and ledgers when you come for dinner."

Roxley slowly nodded. "All right."

"All right?"

"You have my permission to court Athena. Whether or not Charles will give you his is an entirely different matter."

Robert stared at Roxley. He wanted to say that Charles owed him, but the truth of the matter was, he didn't. Not really. Not enough to allow his former friend to romance his sister. Definitely not without Robert making an effort to patch things up between them first. "Would it be possible for me to speak with Charles before I go?"

"I'll ask," Roxley said. He stood and left the room.

When he returned, it was with a furious looking Charles Townsbridge in tow.

"Of all the things I feared you might do to retaliate," Charles said without bothering to offer a greeting, "this is beyond the pale."

"It's good to see you too," Robert said. "And just to be clear, I do not seek to court your sister to get back at you or at her for what happened."

"Court her?" Charles fairly exploded. He swung his gaze toward Roxley. "What the hell is he talking about?"

"I did not have a chance to mention that part yet," Roxely told Robert. "With regard to retaliation, Charles was referring to your holding Athena hostage for the sake of compromising her reputation, as he believes to be the case."

Of course he would. Robert pressed his lips together. "I care for her, Charles."

"I don't believe you."

"Frankly, I don't understand why you wouldn't," Robert snapped. "Have you not met your sister? Do you not realize how wonderful she is?"

Charles opened his mouth, then closed it again. He scratched the back of his head. "You're ten years her senior."

"I am aware of that."

"It's unnatural," Charles grumbled.

"Your mother and I have eleven years between us," Roxley said.

Charles knit his brow and glared at his father. "Not very helpful."

"No. What *would* be helpful," Roxley said, "would be for you to set aside your protective instinct toward Athena and give Darlington a chance. After all, you did steal his bride."

"Which is precisely why I've reason to be suspicious about him suddenly wanting to court my sister." Charles looked at Robert. "You never showed that sort of interest in her before."

Robert choked on the air he was breathing and sputtered slightly. "Good lord, she was only fourteen the last time I saw her. Making advances was the furthest thing from my mind, not simply because I was otherwise engaged but because it would have been utterly inappropriate."

"Duly noted," Charles said after a moment's thought. He took a deep breath, expelled it, and finally took a step closer to Robert. Extending his hand, he said, "I'm very sorry you had to find out about my affection for Bethany on your wedding day. It was wrong. I ought to have told you sooner. Please forgive me, Robert."

Clasping his hand, Robert gave it a firm shake. "Of course."

"Thank you." Charles took a deep breath, then asked, "Shall we call for Athena to join us so you can make your intentions known?"

"I'd rather not," Robert said. He glanced at Roxley. "Your father can explain my reasoning. I believe he agrees with it. As for myself, I really ought to be heading back if I'm to reach home before it gets dark."

"Very well," Charles said. "I'll walk you out."

Robert took his leave of Roxley and went to collect his greatcoat, hat, and gloves. His horse was readied and he stepped out onto the front step together with Charles.

"I'm glad you came," Charles said, then winced. "I'm glad you brought Athena back safe. I'm also glad we had a chance to talk and, I hope, become reacquainted with each other. But you should know that if you harbor any ill-will toward my sister, if you hurt her even the slightest, I will hunt you down and break every bone in your body. Is that clear?"

"Perfectly," Robert told him calmly. Swinging himself up into his saddle, he collected the reins belonging to the horse Athena had ridden, and started his homeward journey.

FOUR CONSECUTIVE DAYS of sunshine had melted most of the snow, allowing the evening out at the assembly hall to proceed as planned. Standing to one side with Sarah and Sarah's husband, the Duke of Brunswick, Athena sipped her punch while watching the country dance in progress. The happy couple had suffered through a rough patch immediately after their wedding and had only been reunited two weeks before joining the rest of the Townsbridges at Foxborough Hall.

"You've been unusually quiet since your return from Darlington House," Sarah said. "Eloise tells me she saw you perched on the windowsill by the stairs this morning."

"I was admiring the view," Athena said.

"For someone who has always been in constant motion, I find that curious."

Athena sighed. "To be honest, I have not been feeling well lately."

Sarah immediately frowned. "Heavens, you should have said something."

"I don't believe it's anything serious, so I saw no reason to worry anyone, but I am beginning to think it would have been best for me to stay home in bed this evening." As it was, a general sense of malaise gripped her body, leaving her with an uncharacteristic feeling of despair.

"Perhaps you ought to sit," Sarah suggested. She helped Athena toward a chair. "Does your head pain you?"

"Not really."

"Your stomach then?"

"Possibly." It certainly didn't feel as it should. Or maybe it was a spot above her stomach that was the problem. Her lungs perhaps, or her heart? She dared not think there might be an issue with either.

"Would you like to return to Foxborough Hall?" Sarah asked.

"And ruin everyone's evening by cutting it short?" Athena shook her head. "Absolutely not. But it might be wise of me to stop drinking this punch."

She set her glass aside. Something disagreed with her, that much was clear. The question was what. Hopefully not the beginnings of a cold, or worse, influenza. She clasped her hands and proceeded to watch the dancing. She'd engaged in a few herself – one with each brother and the last with Brunswick. No other gentleman had invited her onto the floor. Instead, they studied her from a safe distance like timid puppies regarding an unpredictable kitten.

Another set began. Music swirled through the air, drifting up under the ceiling where pine garlands wrapped in red ribbon were strung in honor of the Yuletide season. Couples skipped and twirled. Laughter and chatter mingled with the sort of joyfulness she was wont to welcome. Instead, she wished herself elsewhere – somewhere far away from all the irritating happiness.

"Good heavens," Sarah said at the very same moment Athena decided to step outside for some fresh air. "Did you know he would be here?"

"Who?" she asked, her stomach squeezing tight in anticipation of whom her sister referred to.

"Langdon. I mean, Darlington. He just arrived and...he's coming this way."

Athena stood, her heart pounding with the wild pace of a thousand galloping horses. Her stomach fared no better. It felt like it housed a swarm of butterflies. She glanced in the direction Sarah indicated and instantly sucked in a breath. Sure enough, there he was, handsomer than he'd been four days prior. How was that possible? She did not know and she did not care. All she could do was feel the rush of joy pouring through her while he strode toward her.

"Miss Townsbridge," he murmured as soon as he reached her. "I trust you are having a wonderful evening?"

"Indeed, my lord." Her face grew hot, her insides hotter. What on earth was happening to her?

"Lady Brunswick," he said, addressing Sarah next. "Felicitations on your recent marriage."

"Thank you." Sarah gestured toward her husband. "Have you met the duke before?"

"Indeed I have not," Robert said. He shook Brunswick's hand. "A pleasure."

"Likewise," Brunswick said. "I've heard a great deal about you. Especially during the last few days."

Robert nodded and turned back to Athena. "I'm hoping you might be willing to partner with me for the next set."

"I, um..." Her lungs didn't seem to be working properly. She was having trouble catching her breath. And yet, there was no denying the pure delight he'd instilled in her by asking. So she forced herself to say, "Yes. I'd like that."

Appreciation lit his eyes. The edge of his mouth lifted. "Excellent."

Her brother, Charles, danced past with Bethany, and for a panicked moment, Athena feared an impending altercation. But rather than scowl in response to Robert's presence, Charles acknowledged him with a tilt of his chin before moving on past. Perhaps then they'd already had a chance to speak when Robert was last at Foxborough Hall? If so, Charles hadn't mentioned the encounter.

"I think I'm beginning to figure out what might be ailing you," Sarah whispered close to her ear.

"Really?" Athena met her sister's gaze and was instantly caught off guard by her secretive smile. "What's your theory?"

"I think it might be best if you figure that out on your own," Sarah said with a smirk.

Irritated, Athena prepared to argue that logic when Robert drew her attention. "How long has it been since we last saw each other?"

His voice was low and sensual. Awareness rippled through her. "Four days."

"Is that all?" He leaned in slightly, brushing her arm with his sleeve. "It feels like weeks. Months. Perhaps even years."

She turned her head just enough to meet his gaze. The fire there stole her breath and weakened her knees. Surely he could not mean what she thought he meant. It wasn't possible. She wasn't the sort of person a man would miss, but rather the sort he'd be eager to get rid of. Wasn't that what he'd wanted from the beginning? To get her out of his house as quickly as possible?

Yes. But later, after failing to accomplish that, they'd talked. And as they'd become reacquainted, something had changed. He'd forgiven her. More than that, he'd seemed to accept her.

No. What she'd witnessed was greater than acceptance – a genuine appreciation for her as a person. And while he might have chastised her on occasion, he'd never tried to change who she was. Instead, he'd told her he liked her.

Before she was able to figure out what all this meant, he was leading her onto the dance floor. She took her position across from him, her mind a muddle of contradiction. And then the music was playing and somehow her feet were moving in accordance with the rhythm. A hand caught her waist and spun her around. Heat seared the skin beneath her gown at the point of contact. She drew a shuddering breath and did her best to remain upright.

"You look stunning this evening," Robert murmured, his eyes snaring hers with intense focus. "No other woman compares."

A fluttery feeling spiraled through her. She couldn't speak, could barely think. She certainly had no chance in hell of returning the compliment with panache. And then she lost her opportunity completely as they were forced to switch partners and move in opposite directions. When she returned to Robert's side, he asked if she still liked roast duck, preventing her from returning his praise without risk of sounding utterly daft.

"I do," she said instead. "It's still my favorite food."

"Along with sugar-glazed potatoes and boiled apples filled with red currant jelly?"

A smile curved her lips. "You have a remarkable memory, my lord."

"I've been reflecting," he said with a wink that nearly caused her knees to give way.

They were swept apart once more and before she'd managed to gather her wits, the dance was ending. Robert clasped her hand, spun her gently around one last time, and guided her into her rightful place before stepping back. The final notes faded and he gave her a bow, then led her from the floor in silence.

When they reached the periphery, he drew her toward a vacant corner and raised her gloved hand to his lips. "Until we meet again, Miss Townsbridge."

He was gone before she remembered to breathe.

Chapter Six

EVERYTHING HAD BEEN perfectly thought out. Robert made sure of it. He'd personally overseen the dinner arrangements, ensuring Athena would be seated directly to his left and her mother to his right. After their dance the other evening at the assembly hall, he'd scarcely slept a wink. He'd been horribly nervous and unsure when he'd arrived. After all, it would be clear to anyone paying attention that he'd come solely to dance with her. And yet the moment he was in her company, he had relaxed and found the right words. Whether or not she knew it, she had responded to his flirtation with rosy cheeks and an uncharacteristically timid smile. Both allowed him to hope.

"Is the duck to your liking?" he asked Athena once she'd had a chance to savor the food.

"It is delicious." she assured him, her gaze not quite meeting his while she ate a bit more. Her low voice and high color, however, told him she wasn't indifferent. Something else was causing her to shy away. Perhaps the dawning realization that they could be more than friends?

"I believe it is your favorite," Lady Roxley said.

"It is." Athena set her knife and fork aside and reached for her glass. She took a sip and, without another word, continued eating.

"How fortuitous," Lady Roxley said. She gave Robert an assessing look, added a wry smile, and swiftly changed the subject.

Half an hour later, Robert had been fully informed of the Townsbridges' plans for the rest of the holiday season. They would depart for London three days hence so they could return in time to attend the yearly Christmas concert at the Theatre Royal. Christmas itself would be celebrated at Townsbridge House with a large family dinner and a variety of games. According to her ladyship, New Year's Eve was generally spent there as well, but this year they intended to head to Vauxhall and watch the firework display. Provided the weather permitted, of course.

"Tea has been prepared in the parlor," Dartwood announced once the meal was over.

Athena leapt to her feet, nearly knocking over her chair in the process.

"Dear me," her mother exclaimed. "Do be careful."

"Forgive me," Athena murmured while everyone else stood. "It seems my eagerness to enjoy a hot beverage has made me forget my manners."

Deciding it was best to remain silent, Robert simply inclined his head and watched her hasten away. The other ladies followed, until he was left alone with her father, her brothers, the Duke of Brunswick and the Marquess of Foxborough.

"I've never seen Athena so out of sorts before," James said with a grin. "It's refreshing."

"Do you suppose she knows she's in love yet?" Brunswick asked.

Everyone turned to stare at him. Robert's heart slammed against his chest. "In love?"

The duke gave him a knowing smile. "She has not been herself since she returned from your home, but rather quiet and distant. According to what she told my wife, she felt unwell. Until you showed up at the assembly hall and she started to glow. If I were to hazard a guess, being apart from you caused her distress."

"Then why was she so eager to leave his company moments ago?" Foxborough asked.

Charles snorted. "Because she doesn't understand her feelings. Athena has always been a force to be reckoned with, only now, she has become the victim of something more powerful than herself. Her instinct will likely be to fight it, and when she discovers she can't, she'll finally surrender to the truth. Or at least, that is my theory."

Robert wondered if his friend was right and if so, how long Athena's surrender might take.

"Have you considered being direct with her?" William asked. "I'm thinking it might make everything a lot simpler."

"Perhaps with someone besides Athena," Robert said. "When it comes to her, instinct tells me she needs time to acquaint herself with the idea of having gained a man's attention. From what I understand, she's not used to it, so too strong an advance on my part might push her away."

"Well, you have our support," Lord Roxley said. "We are all of the opinion that you would be good for her."

"Provided your intentions are as honorable as you claim," Charles said.

A wave of anger rolled through Robert, pushing at his nerves. Of course, it made sense for Charles to still doubt him. All Robert could do was continue to offer assurance.

"I promise you they are." Robert held Charles's gaze for a moment before giving his attention to Viscount Roxley. "My lord, if you would please follow me to my study, I'll show you my ledgers and whatever else you need to see in order to form an accurate opinion of my finances."

Two hours later, Robert's guests took their leave. He'd not had a chance to converse with Athena at greater length, but he had obtained her father's approval along with permission to call on his daughter whenever he pleased.

"Watch the steps," William said as he escorted his wife toward one of three awaiting carriages. "It's a frosty night. There could be ice."

The rest of the Townsbridges moved forward with care, the ladies allowing their husbands to offer support.

"Wait here a moment while I help your mother," Lord Roxley told Athena. "It won't take but a moment."

"You need not worry over me, Papa," Athena replied as she started to follow her parents. "I have excellent balance."

"Athena," Robert said, grabbing her arm before she was able to take one more step. "I know you're sturdy on your feet, but there's no sense in being reckless."

"Of course not," she quickly agreed. "I just—"

"Allow me to walk you to your conveyance." He drew her nearer to his side and was pleased to feel her relax against his hold.

"Thank you, my lord."

Robert answered her with a smile, then guided her down the stone steps, pausing here and there in order to test them for slippery spots.

They reached the carriage, but rather than hand her up, he turned her toward him. "If you will permit, I should like to call upon you in London."

Her lips parted, but this time, instead of glancing away, her eyes held his with unblinking alertness. She sucked in a breath and for a moment she seemed to stand at the edge of a cliff, unsure of whether or not to jump. But then she raised her chin and something changed. Her expression softened, and a smile captured her lips as she said, "Nothing would please me more."

Joy filled his heart to the point of bursting. Not caring if it was appropriate or not, he took a step closer and lowered his head, brushing her cheek with his lips. "I'm glad."

She clasped his hand, squeezing it gently as if to convey her accord. Without saying anything further, he helped her up, unable to stop from grinning when she raised her hem and he caught a flash of brown buckskin leather. Even in her evening finery, Athena was every bit the hoyden he'd fallen in love with.

KEEPING A FIRM HOLD of her niece's and nephew's hands, Athena helped them keep their balance while skating the length of the Serpentine. They were both improving. She wasn't nearly as worried about them falling as she'd been last year when they'd tested their skates for the very first time.

"There's a vendor over there selling roasted chestnuts," she said. "Would you like some?"

"Oh yes," Lilly exclaimed.

"Do you think he's got mince pies too?" Lucas asked.

"I don't know," Athena told him. "We'll have to see."

They skated toward the embankment and took a seat on the benches to remove their skates. As it turned out, the vendor had not only mince pies and chestnuts, but squares of Christmas cake too. Deciding to ignore Charles's warning about not spoiling the children's appetites, Athena bought one of each item for them to share. Aware they needed to keep their hands free for eating, she grabbed their skates and started escorting them back toward Hyde Park Corner.

Keeping busy was the only way for her to retain her sanity these days. As soon as she stopped moving, her thoughts would return to every conversation she and Robert had shared. Especially the last one. Her heart raced when she recalled his words and the kiss he'd bestowed upon her cheek. Everything made sense now. She finally understood the misery she'd experienced after returning to Foxborough Hall and why her spirits had been renewed when she'd seen Robert again. She also knew why she'd felt so out of breath in his presence, why her skin had heated with prickly awareness, and why her stomach had tied itself into knots.

She longed for him, and yet his nearness had made her unspeakably nervous. Because she loved him, and for once in her life another person's opinion – his opinion – mattered. She was terrified he might think her a fool, that she'd be her usual self and say something rash – something that would remind him she wasn't suited to be a wife, never mind a marchioness.

And yet, the way he'd looked at her left no doubt in her mind. He genuinely liked her, just the way she was.

"Aunt Athena?" Lilly's voice penetrated her thoughts. "My laces are undone. Can you please tie them?"

Athena blinked. "Of course."

She crouched before her niece and proceeded with the task. As she finished tying the bow with a double knot for good measure, she heard footsteps approach. Glancing sideways, she spotted the gleam of expensive men's boots, instinctively looked up, and froze. Every emotion she'd gone through during the course of the last month exploded inside her.

"Miss Townsbridge," Robert murmured. "Your family butler said I would find you here."

He held his hand toward her and as she took it and he helped her rise, she could have sworn she saw sparks fly between their fingers. It felt like the air had been squeezed from her lungs and as though her heart had taken flight. "Lord Darlington."

"Robert," he insisted, his eyes bright with a hint of mischief.

She swallowed and managed a quick polite curtsey. "My niece and nephew, Miss Lilly and Master Lucas."

"Charles and Bethany's children?"

"Indeed," Athena said, suddenly apprehensive of the introduction.

If Robert harbored any lingering regrets, he showed no sign of it. Instead, he smiled at Lilly and Lucas. "It is a pleasure to make your acquaintances."

Lilly extended her hand. "Would you like a chestnut?"

"How kind of you to offer," Robert told her with an indulgent grin. He selected a chestnut and quickly ate it. "These are excellent. The best I've ever had."

Lilly beamed at him as if he were the sun and the stars. Lucas, who was that bit older than his sister, frowned. "What sort of lord are you?"

"I'm a marquess."

"Hmm." Lucas glanced at Athena, then back at Robert. "Do you wish to marry our aunt?"

Athena choked on the air she'd been breathing and instantly coughed. "Lucas!"

The boy, every bit as serious as his papa, merely shrugged. "As your only male relative here, I should know his intentions."

"Quite right," Robert chuckled. Amusement danced in his eyes. "And the answer is yes. If she'll have me."

Everything came to a standstill. Athena blinked. Had Robert just said what she thought he'd said? Surely not. She tried to breathe, tried to feel the ground beneath her feet. "That's not a...I mean, you didn't just...Robert, are you—"

"No."

"No?"

"That was not a proposal, but rather an assurance to satisfy Master Lucas's concerns."

"I see." Athena stared at him. She felt like she had been hung upside down. The world wasn't quite as steady as it had been before Robert's arrival.

Lilly took a massive bite from the mince pie. "I'm cold. Can we keep walking?"

"Of course," Athena said.

"It's good to see you again," Robert said as he fell into step beside her.

Taking courage, Athena reached out and took his arm. "Likewise."

They proceeded in silence for a while before Robert said, "I hope you know why I'm here."

"Considering you've not been to Town in years, I'm guessing it must involve a matter of great importance."

"Indeed it does." His hand covered hers, the warmth there infusing her skin. "I am hoping we will have a chance to discuss it in private when we arrive at Townsbridge House."

"I am sure that can be arranged," she said, offering him the assurance she thought he might need. Beneath her hand, she felt his muscles flex, and when she looked up, she saw the strain in his features. This was not a man at ease but rather one strung tight with tension.

Her own stomach tightened in response, her pulse leaping with every step they took, until they reached their destination and stepped inside the house. The children quickly removed their outerwear garments and hurried through to the parlor so they could relate the details of their excursion to their grandparents.

Athena untied her bonnet and handed it to the butler before removing her cloak and gloves. Robert followed suit, dispensing with his greatcoat and hat.

"This way." Athena grabbed his hand and pulled him toward the back of the house. She opened the door to the library, swept the space with her gaze, and stepped inside. "Here we are. The privacy you requested, my lord."

He followed her into the room and shut the door.

Athena glanced at it, then at him. A fluttery feeling erupted within her breast. Never in her life had she been subjected to such unfeigned yearning. Good heavens, the man was looking at her as if he'd not eaten for years and intended her to be his next meal.

"Robert?" His name whispered across her lips.

He moved toward her. A nerve ticked at the edge of his jaw. Swallowing, he reached for her hand. "You wrecked everything for me six years ago, and yet, although you had no reason to believe I harbored anything else but anger toward you, you still sought me out in an effort to make amends. Athena, you are tempestuous, willful, and more than capable of testing my sanity, but you're also spirited, strong, and utterly wonderful. And while I must confess I never imagined falling in love with you, I have. My heart is yours and I am hoping, praying, that yours is mine as well, for if it is not, then—"

"It is." Tears of joy dampened her eyes as she spoke. She raised his hand to her lips and pressed a reverent kiss to his knuckles. "I am yours."

"Then marry me. Be my wife, my marchioness. Allow me to guide you, to cherish your bright disposition, and to adore you."

"I have a better idea." When concern stole into his gaze she hastened to say, "Let us guide, cherish, and adore each other."

A flare of intensity turning his eyes a bright shade of blue was her only warning before she was swept into his arms. His mouth found hers, and he kissed her with such searing passion she felt herself scorched. It was as if a lifelong attempt at restraint had been undone within a heartbeat. Gone was the gentleman he'd been as long as she'd known him, replaced by a would-be scoundrel intent on branding her with his kiss.

Athena gasped as she wound her arms around his neck and welcomed the deep caress. She'd never been subjected to such intense passion before, had never believed herself capable of instilling such powerful feeling in any man. She realized now that all it took was the right man. Robert. As unexpected and unlikely, he was her perfect match. And he loved her. Fiercely, if the ardor with which he kissed her was any indication.

His mouth stole over her cheek, then down the side of her neck. "My God. I am the luckiest man alive."

She chuckled slightly in response. "I'm not sure other men would agree. From what I gather, I am an acquired taste."

He raised his head, the look in his eyes so stormy she scarcely knew what to make of it. His hand cupped her cheek and then he told her sternly, "They're fools. All of them. As far as I am concerned, I've snatched up the only diamond the world has to offer."

Speechless, she welcomed the next kiss he gave her. It was more languid than the first – a promise made with the slow press of his lips against hers. "I love you. Don't ever doubt that."

"I won't."

He pulled her into a tight embrace and simply held her a moment. When he released her again, he looked calmer than she'd seen him since she'd stormed into his home and demanded he hear her out.

"Are you ready to announce our engagement?" he asked.

She nodded. "The sooner the better, so we can get on with planning the wedding."

With a grin, he swept her back into his arms and kissed her again.

NEW YEAR'S EVE CAME and went in a blur of wedding preparations. As soon as everyone knew Athena and Robert intended to marry, Athena had no time to herself whatsoever. Every second of every day was filled with visits to various shops: florists, milliners, confectioners, modistes, haberdashers, and even goldsmiths. Never in her life had she imagined how much work went into becoming a wife. According to her mother, her sister, and her three sisters-in-law, she needed monogrammed bed sheets and towels, new day dresses and evening gowns. When Athena protested, they told her the clothes she currently owned wouldn't do.

"You shall be a married woman," Sarah said, "and as such, you will be permitted to wear brighter colors."

Athena could only sigh while the whirlwind continued around her. There were silk chemises and velvet robes, embroidered stockings trimmed with Belgian lace and ribbon, stays crafted from slippery satin, and they'd not even started discussing her wedding gown. It was exhausting.

Drumming her fingers against a bolt of fabric while her mother informed the third dressmaker they'd seen in the space of a week of a riding habit that simply had to be ready within the next fortnight, Athena decided she'd had enough. This wasn't her, and she was fairly certain Robert wouldn't give two figs about seeing her trussed up in some feminine concoction fit for a courtesan. But she believed there might be something else he'd like.

So she stood and went to join her mother. She waited patiently for her to finish the description of all the frog closures she wanted to line the front of Athena's jacket, how they had to match the trim and the black feather in the ridiculous hat she wanted to order, before telling the modiste, "Since my mother insists upon this order, you must make it, even if I have no intention of ever putting it on."

"Athena," her mother hissed.

"I do not ride sidesaddle, Mama, and what you're describing would be incredibly impractical for anything else."

"But—"

"All I want is a shirt."

"A shirt?" her mother sputtered.

"Madame," Athena said, addressing the modiste, "I have a penchant for wearing breeches. From what I have gathered, my future husband likes the way I look in them, so a shirt – something light and airy, cut in a masculine style but with a feminine touch meant to entice, would be splendid."

The dressmaker gave her a sly smile. "A translucent white muslin shirt with stays to match would surely entice any man. Perhaps with a sleeveless gown worn over it. I trust your breeches are snug?"

"I have them on underneath my dress so I can easily show you," Athena said with a grin while her mother groaned in horror. "If you think you can make a better pair, I'll happily add it to my order."

Two weeks later, Athena met Robert for a walk in the park. He'd visited Townsbridge House a number of times for dinner, but this was a chance for them to speak more freely, without her family hovering nearby. Instead, a maid followed at a respectable distance.

"I cannot wait for this precise hour the day after tomorrow," she said, "because then you and I shall be married, and the hell I've been subjected to these past few weeks will be over."

"Has it really been so bad?" he asked.

She gave him a dry look. "We ought to trade places and then revisit that question."

He grinned. "Just wait until my mother arrives tomorrow. I'm sure she'll want to take you out too. In fact, she writes that she's very excited to see you again."

Athena winced. She'd not seen the dowager marchioness since being ushered out of her home with several heartfelt apologies spoken from Athena's father. "Do you truly think so?"

His arm wound around her and pulled her close in a show of affection that wasn't the least bit proper in public. Certainly not by an unmarried couple. "With Papa gone, her greatest wish is for me to be happy."

"Will she be staying at Mivart's as well?" Athena asked in reference to the hotel. Since Robert had let the London mansion he'd been bequeathed as part of his inheritance, he'd chosen to rent a room for the duration of his stay in London.

"No. She prefers to visit with her sister instead."

"You do not wish to join her?"

"As fond as I am of my aunt, she would only want to dictate every hour of my day. Staying at Mivart's allows me to retain my independence. And privacy."

"Ah," Athena sighed. "How I envy the privilege of being a man."

"And how delighted I am by the fact that you're not one." He chuckled. Threading his fingers between hers he raised her hand, pushed back her glove, and placed a heated kiss against her wrist. "Lord help me but I can scarcely wait for us to be wed."

Happier than she'd ever been, Athena served him her brightest smile just as a plump drop of water splattered against her cheek. "Oh!"

"Hmm... Looks like it's starting to rain. We should probably head back toward the carriage."

No sooner had he made the suggestion then the clouds opened and water pelted down in a torrent. Something large and heavy landed across Athena's shoulders. Robert had shucked his greatcoat, grabbed her hand, and was marching her along while she did her best to keep up. A swift glance over her shoulder assured her that her maid was not far behind.

Huddled beneath the much-too-large garment while water fell over the brim of her bonnet, Athena pressed closer to Robert as they hurried toward the park entrance. Townsbridge House wasn't far from there, but caught in the middle of a torrential downpour, it might as well have been miles away. By the time they arrived, they were all soaked through, although Athena was slightly dryer thanks to Robert's chivalrousness.

"Dear me," Athena's mother said when she met them in the foyer. "We need to get you warmed up and dried off right away. Lord Darlington, I can have the maids prepare a hot bath for you while we send for a change of clothes."

"Thank you, my lady, for your generosity, but it would be easier for me to return directly to Mivart's and dry off there, without imposing upon your servants." He swung his sopping wet greatcoat over his shoulders and looked to Athena. "A pleasure as always, my love. When we meet again it will be in front of the vicar."

"I can scarcely wait."

"Neither can I." He placed a damp palm against her cheek.

"You're freezing," Athena gasped. "Are you sure you don't want to accept Mama's offer?"

"Like you, I've a great deal to see to before the wedding. I must be off." He held her gaze for a moment, then turned back toward her mother and gave her his thanks once more before striding out into the storm.

Chapter Seven

A LETTER FROM ROBERT arrived the following day, inquiring after Athena's health. She wrote back, informing him she was well, that her wedding gown had arrived, and that she was more than ready for them to begin their life together.

When Athena woke the next morning, ice crystals had formed on her window. She pressed her fingertips against the frozen glass. They'd not picked the best time of year for a wedding, but at least today was clear without a hint of rain. A maid started a fire in the grate while another brought Athena a hot cup of tea and a breakfast tray.

"Are you ready to get dressed?" her mother asked a short while later when she came to check on her.

Athena popped the last of her toast in her mouth and savored the sweet cherry preserves she'd scooped onto it. "I believe so."

Her mother smiled and stepped aside to grant the small parade of maids waiting outside entry. Just as it had been on that long ago day when she'd been presented at court, her body was washed from head to toe before being perfumed. Hair was pulled, braided, styled, and adorned with diamond-tipped pins, and her face was massaged with a milky honey-scented lotion before being powdered. Stockings were tied in place with ribbons, a silk chemise slipped over her head. Then came the stays and at last the gown itself. Lace cap sleeves with scalloped edging embroidered with silver thread accentuated the pleated simplicity of the bodice. A wide satin ribbon circled her waist, below which the skirt fell in light diaphanous folds.

"You look stunning," her mother said. "Let's hope you don't render your future husband too speechless. After all, he still has to speak his vows."

With a grin, Athena accompanied her downstairs where her father stood waiting. A sheen of moisture brightened his eyes the moment he saw her. "Good lord. I'm starting to wonder if there's any man on this earth who deserves you."

"Robert does," Athena told him.

"You're quite certain?" her father asked, as if to be sure.

"More than I've ever been about anything else before."

Leaning forward, her father placed a kiss upon her cheek. "Then by all means, let us be off so you can have him."

Wrapped in a cloak she intended to take off when they reached the church, Athena savored the warmth of the hot brick placed at her feet in the carriage. St. James's Church wasn't far. It took them no more than five minutes to reach it. Carriages and horses belonging to guests packed the streets around the building. Filled with excitement, Athena alit from her own conveyance and started forward, following her parents inside.

But when she entered the vestibule, she was met by Charles, William, and James, who all looked unnervingly grim. Athena's heart made a small flutter.

"He's not here yet," Charles declared without any preamble.

Athena stared at her brother, who looked about ready to pummel someone. "How late is he?"

"He was supposed to be here ten minutes ago at the latest. Everyone else was." Charles crossed his arms and glared at her as if Robert's absence was somehow her fault.

Athena scowled right back. "Something has clearly delayed him. Go back inside, show Mama and Papa to their seats, and tell the vicar to wait."

"Might I say, you look incredibly lovely," William told her.

"Yes," Charles clipped. "A pity Darlington isn't here to see it."

"He will be," Athena informed him.

James cleared his throat. "What if—"

"No." Athena gave her brothers and her parents a firm look. "We are going to wait. That is all."

Charles puffed out a breath, then gave a swift nod of agreement. "Very well. But if he's not here within five minutes, I'll skewer him myself."

Turning her back on her irate brother, Athena crossed her arms and faced the door in anticipation of Robert's arrival. Why wasn't he here yet? If something had caused a delay, surely he would have sent word. Unease crept under her skin. Something must have happened. He wouldn't just leave her like this. Would he?

Athena stared out into the wintry street beyond. It would be the perfect retaliation. Closing her eyes, she tried to ignore the whispers coming from within the church. Some were not as discreet as she would have liked. A pang of despair caught her heart. Robert had not deserted her. She refused to believe it. No one could be so convincing in their display of love and affection as he without its being real.

"It's been five minutes." Charles's voice caused her to flinch. "Needless to say, people are starting to wonder about his absence."

"They believe I've been jilted," Athena said as she turned toward him.

"It would not be an unreasonable assumption to make."

Athena straightened her spine and clenched her jaw. "Stop it, Charles. Robert is your friend. Have some faith in him."

"He *was* my friend, and while I will admit it was I who wronged him, the blow he has dealt this family in return is so low, I shall never forgive him for it. How dare he do this to you? And how could I have allowed myself to believe he wouldn't?"

Anger flared to life within Athena so swiftly it almost choked her. Balling her hands into fists she glared into her brother's eyes. "If Robert has indeed plotted revenge in this manner, then it is nothing less than I deserve. But the Robert I know would not be so cruel, and frankly, it astounds me to discover that you imagine he would."

"Athena, I—"

"No. I refuse to believe him capable of it until I hear him confess it himself. Until then, I must believe something else has kept him away. And right now, I have every intention of finding out what it might be."

"You're leaving?" he asked when she started back toward the carriage she'd arrived in.

"I have to find him, Charles."

"But what about all the guests?"

"They will spread their vicious gossip no matter what we do. I, for one, have no intention of staying here to listen to it."

"I should accompany you," he said.

She glanced at him while considering his proposal. "Fine. As long as you swear not to harm him in any way once we find him."

"Very well. You have my word. Just give me a minute to tell Bethany where I've gone."

Athena continued toward the carriage while he raced back to the church. She'd just climbed in and arranged her skirts when he returned.

"Was Robert's mother present?" Athena asked once they were headed to Mivart's.

"She was."

Athena nodded. "Then all the more reason not to imagine the worst of him. He'd never subject her to scandal."

"He's a lucky fellow," Charles muttered. "I'm not sure many other women would have been equally ready to defend their fiancés in such a situation."

Athena turned her gaze toward the window. She would find out what had happened before passing judgment, but if she did learn Robert had played her false, she would challenge him to a bloody duel. Not in defense of her own honor, but because her poor parents did not deserve to be put through another disgraceful ordeal.

But when she arrived at the hotel and inquired after him, the clerk at the front desk informed her that he'd not seen Lord Darlington since the previous day. "He had his dinner brought up to his room. Before the maid left, he told her he wanted an early night and asked not to be disturbed."

"And you have not checked on him since?" Athena asked with growing concern.

"It's not unusual for our guests to rise later in the day. Many of them are out until the early hours of the morning and—"

"I need a key," Athena said. "To his suite of rooms."

The clerk blanched. "I cannot provide you with that."

"Then prepare to have every door kicked in until we find him," Charles said.

"My lord." The clerk's eyes darted between them both. Realizing they were serious, he quickly collected a key and hastened toward the stairs. "I shall escort you."

Athena picked up the hem of her gown and hurried after him with Charles immediately on her heels. When they reached the second floor, the clerk turned right and walked briskly toward the door at the end. Athena rather wished he would run.

"Lord Darlington?" the clerk called after giving the door a knock. "Are you there?"

"Does he not have a valet with him?' Charles asked Athena. "Someone to send word if he was unwell?"

Athena raised her own fist and gave the door three loud raps. "Not everyone can afford such luxury, Charles. Robert has been trying to save the expense of unnecessary staff."

"I see."

When no one responded from inside the room, Athena said, "Open the door."

"But—"

"Oh, for heaven's sake." She snatched the key from the clerk and thrust it into the lock. One second later she crossed the threshold and froze. The room was eerily dark with curtains still drawn. And there was a sound – a raspy sort of breathing coming from within the adjoining bedchamber. Leaping across the floor, Athena dashed to Robert's side. "Bloody hell and a thousand damnations!"

"Athena, you shouldn't—"

"Don't you dare tell me what I should or should not do," Athena snapped at her brother. Tears stung her eyes as her throat clogged with emotion. "Fetch the damn physician if you want to make yourself useful."

"I merely wished to say that you probably shouldn't get too close to him. He's obviously deathly ill and I'd hate for you to—"

"Just go," she sobbed as she pressed her palm to Robert's scorching hot forehead. "Now!"

He was barely out the door before she'd located a handkerchief. After wetting it in the washbasin, she spread it across Robert's brow. He groaned softly in response, drawing her attention to his chapped lips. Unsure of how to help him drink when he was lying down and barely lucid, she found another handkerchief and, after soaking it, attempted to squeeze the water into his mouth. He groaned again, though she wasn't sure whether the sound he made was one of gratitude or irritation.

Tucking the covers around him, she made sure he was properly covered by his blanket, then went to open the window. The room was too stuffy. The sickly smell filling it would not improve anyone's health. Of course, it was freezing outside, so she had to take care that letting a bit of crisp air inside did not make him worse.

Athena glanced at the fire burning in the grate, added a log, and turned to the clerk who still stood near the door. Uncertainty marred his features. "Some tea please, along with some honey and a bowl of hot soup, if you have it."

"We have one with ox tail and one with chicken," he said, shifting his feet. "Which would you prefer?"

"Bring up the chicken soup, please. Strained so the meat and vegetables are separate from the liquid."

"I'll see to it right away." The clerk left.

Athena returned to Robert's bedside, checked the compress and, finding it warm, went to soak it again in cool water before returning it to his forehead.

His eyes blinked in response to her touch. "Drink."

She poured some water into a glass, did her best to raise him into more of a sitting position, and held the glass to his lips. With trembling hands, he clasped it, and drank. His eyes opened wider, into a squint. "Athena?"

"Yes, my love. I'm here."

"Should be at church," he told her hoarsely. "Must get married."

"Hush now and rest. We'll get married later."

A wheezing snore was his only response. He'd already fallen back asleep. Athena lowered his head to the pillow and set the glass aside. Where was the blasted physician? She clamped her jaw tightly and fought the urge to cry, but in spite of her stalwart attempts, tears still rolled down her cheeks. *Please*, she prayed, *don't leave me now*. She lay down next to Robert's body and held on for all she was worth.

It felt like forever before Charles returned. He brought with him a man who introduced himself as Dr. Donovan.

Athena stared at the much-too-young physician a moment before addressing her brother. "Where is Dr. Farendale?"

"Away for the next two weeks, according to his housekeeper."

Athena's heart sank. The Townsbridge family physician was a man she trusted implicitly. He'd cared for her every time she'd been sick, and she wanted him to care for Robert too. Despair swept through her. Dr. Donovan didn't look like he was one day older than she, which to her frame of mind was cause for great alarm.

Additional tears pooled against her lashes. "It is imperative to me that Robert survives."

"I know that," Charles told her, his voice conveying a calm she could not comprehend at the moment. He glanced at the only option he'd brought. "Dr. Donovan cared for Lilly and Lucas earlier this year when they came down with a bout of chickenpox. He is a competent man. Please give him a chance."

"Fine." Athena looked at the youth who stood wavering near the door. It wasn't as if she had much choice. "Please examine my fiancé and let me know what I am to do in order to help him recover."

Dipping his head in acknowledgement, Dr. Donovan moved to the bed and sniffed the air. Athena sank onto a nearby chair with a bleak sigh. She'd have been better off trying to haul Robert to the nearest hospital. She watched with decreasing hope as Dr. Donovan went through the motion of checking Robert's forehead, feeling his pulse, and listening to his breathing.

When he eventually straightened and took a step back from the bed, his expression was grim. "I believe his lordship has influenza."

Athena had suspected as much, but having someone verify her opinion caused her insides to wilt in a way she'd never experienced before. The disease was too often deadly.

Still, the physician could be wrong, could he not? Perhaps all this was, was a serious cold. Unwilling to accept his prognosis, Athena asked him directly, "Do you even possess a university education?"

Dr. Donovan gave her a frank stare. "I studied medicine in Edinburgh for five years, during which I apprenticed under Sir Charles Bell."

"Well then." Athena gave the young physician a grudging frown. "How would you advise us to proceed?"

"Unfortunately, there is very little we can do besides make him comfortable, ensure he eats, drinks, and receives as much rest as possible. Sleep, sustenance, and keeping his temperature down are the only remedies. The rest will be up to him."

Jaw tight, Athena clenched her fists and stood. She wanted to throw something at the useless fellow, scream and rail at him until she was hoarse.

"Athena," Charles warned as if sensing her state of deteriorating calmness, "Dr. Donovan did have to leave a luncheon meeting in order to come here, and having Robert's condition confirmed is surely of some use."

She nodded, thanked the physician, and went to help the maid who'd just arrived with a tray filled exactly with what Athena had ordered. Finally, someone who knew how to step in and do what their profession demanded. Athena turned to her brother. "Please let the rest of our family know what is going on. Robert's mother will need to be informed as well."

"I'll return to help as soon as it's done, so I can be here to offer assistance."

"No," Athena told him. "You have children. Exposing you to this illness more than necessary would be reckless. I'll send word if I need anything."

"Are you sure?" Charles didn't look remotely convinced.

"Dr. Donovan," Athena said. "Would you please inform my brother that there is no reason for two of us to risk our health by remaining here?"

"Indeed, it would be prudent to minimize contact with the patient as much as possible," he said.

"There you are, Charles. Go home and let me deal with this."

"You're sure you can manage?"

"Absolutely."

With another hesitant glance at Robert's slumbering form, Charles gave a reluctant nod and departed with the physician. Athena took a fortifying breath and crossed to the table where the maid had left the tray. Picking up the bowl of broth, she returned to the bed, perched herself on the edge of it, and prepared to wake Robert just long enough for him to eat.

With careful movements, she spooned broth into his mouth. He thanked her and begged for cold water to drink, which she gave him.

"Athena, dearest. Is there anything I can do to help?" her mother asked when she came to bring a change of clothes later that evening. She wasn't alone but had brought Robert's mother with her. "You look a wreck."

"I'm fine, Mama," Athena lied because truthfully, she'd never been more afraid in her life. She gave Lady Darlington a hesitant look. "I'm sorry I didn't come to inform you of Robert's illness myself, but I was reluctant to leave his side."

"You made the right decision," Lady Darlington assured her.

"We thought we might stay here with you," Mama said.

Athena shook her head. "Charles already offered to do the same. I sent him away."

"Well, you're not getting rid of me," Mama informed her.

"Nor me," Lady Darlington added.

"I see no reason for either of you to risk your health," Athena countered. "I do not want you getting sick too. You ought to go home."

Her mother crossed her arms and held her position. "It isn't proper for you to be here by yourself with an unmarried man."

"As far as I am concerned," Athena exploded, her fear causing her to abandon all reason, "we are husband and wife. I'll not let a vicar or a signature stand in the way of my caring for him. I'll not leave his side."

A sob wracked her body and she helplessly buried her face in her hands, ashamed of the weakened state she'd been reduced to. This wasn't her. She was the strong one, the one who barged through life with the constant conviction that things would turn out as they should. Except right now, she wasn't sure of anything anymore, and she very much feared Robert wouldn't survive this. He was a strong man, and yet he was so incredibly weak at the moment – could barely speak, never mind eat or drink.

Her mother's arms came around her and for the first time in years, she allowed herself to accept the support being offered. "I understand, Athena. Lord help me, I understand you better than you can imagine."

"I know, Mama." Her mother had lost a child once to smallpox. Claire had been Sarah's twin.

"You are doing what you can," Lady Darlington added.

"I want to do more."

"Right now," Mama said, "he needs rest, something to eat and drink when he's able, and for you to keep his temperature down. There's nothing more to be done besides waiting to see how he fares."

Athena gulped a breath and nodded. It was what Dr. Donovan had told her, but somehow her mother's soothing voice made it sound much more reasonable. "All right."

"We'll take shifts." Lady Darlington's voice brooked no argument, and as Athena reminded herself, she had every right to stay and help look after her son. "This could last a week so you will need rest as well."

"We promise to wake you if he asks for you or if his condition changes," Mama said. "Agreed?"

"Yes." Athena stepped back and reached for her mother's hand. She held on tight. "Thank you. Both of you"

In spite of the two women's subsequent protest, Athena watched Robert that night while her mother and Lady Darlington slept on the sofas in the next room. When she checked Robert's compress later, it was warm.

"This is what Hell must feel like," he groaned during one of his more wakeful moments that night. "My eyes are on fire."

Locating additional handkerchiefs, Athena wet them all and hung them by the partially open window in the hope that the added winter air would make them cooler. It seemed to work, but when Robert's fever continued to rise the following evening, even they heated up mere seconds after being placed on his skin.

Unsure what else to do, Athena sat and held his hand while he tossed and turned. She wiped his brow, changed the compresses, and made sure he drank plenty of water.

"It's time for you to sleep," Lady Darlington informed her when dawn brought a dim light into the room. "Your mother and I will watch over him until you wake."

"I really don't want to leave him."

"I know, but you'll be of more use to him if you're well-rested instead of bleary-eyed and exhausted. Trust me, Athena, I know what I'm doing."

Accepting her Lady Darlington's advice, Athena bent to press a soft kiss against Robert's brow before going to find the vacant sofa. She collapsed with a sigh and slept one second later. It was a process that continued until she lost track of the days. Everything had become one big blur of endless time, stretching in both directions. With the help of some maids, Athena and the two other ladies managed to change Robert's bed sheets a couple of times after they were soaked through with sweat.

Athena's heart ached as she sat in the chair next to his bed, ready to keep vigil again. Another fresh bowl of broth had been delivered along with some tea and honey. Deciding to change his compress before attempting to feed him again, she collected the handkerchief pressed to his brow and brushed her fingertips gently across his skin.

A bright spark of hope darted through her. She sucked in a breath and placed her palm over his forehead. The heat she'd felt there before had retreated, thank God.

Allowing a smile for the first time in days, she forced back the tears of joy creeping into her eyes and returned to her seat. Best let him sleep. With the fever gone, she was certain he'd wake on his own when he was ready to eat.

"Athena?"

The low, rough sound of her name and a gentle pull on her hand roused her from her slumber. She started and scrambled upright in her chair with a gasp. Her gaze darted about the room until she realized it was Robert who'd spoken. He was watching her with a steady gaze that sent instant relief crashing through her.

"You're awake," she whispered and checked his forehead again to be sure the fever was indeed gone.

"I'm sorry to disturb you," he said, "but I'm so incredibly thirsty. And hungry."

A grin caught her lips as she leapt from her chair. "Yes. Of course. You've barely had anything to eat or drink in days."

She filled a glass with water and helped Robert into a sitting position, this time with greater ease than before now that he was able to help get himself upright. He took the glass from her and downed the liquid while she called for a maid to bring up a proper bowl of soup and some bread. As soon as the meal arrived, he ate with gusto until no drop remained.

A yawn followed. "I think I'll sleep a bit more now if that's all right."

"Of course," Athena assured him. She tucked the blankets around his shoulders and kissed the top of his head. "I'm so incredibly glad to see you looking better."

"I love you," he murmured.

"I love you too."

Chapter Eight

IT TOOK ANOTHER WEEK before Robert began feeling like his old self. Christ, he'd been sick. The fact that he scarcely recalled anything beyond vague visions of people moving about the room and distant voices conversing was testament to the half-conscious state he'd been in. His rooms had now been completely aired out. Five days had passed since Athena had returned home with Lady Roxley. He missed her terribly, but they'd both needed time to recover and the small reprieve had allowed him to spend some time with his mother, for which he was grateful.

Donning his hat and gloves, he prepared to leave Mivart's for the first time in a fortnight. Lord and Lady Roxley had invited him to dine, providing he felt up to it, and he'd happily accepted the invitation. When he arrived, he was glad to discover that it would be a small, intimate family dinner, without the rest of the Townsbridges present.

"I'm sorry I ruined our wedding," he told Athena softly once the initial greetings had been concluded. "Are you certain you still want me, after everything I've put you through?"

She stared at him as if she failed to comprehend the words coming out of his mouth. "After everything *you* put *me* through? How about everything I put you through, Robert?

You suffered years of torment because of me. As for your influenza, I was more than happy to make sure you survived it. Good lord, I love you, you daft man."

"And I love you, you brazen vixen," he said with a grin. "The headlines do too, it would seem. This morning you were mentioned as the lady who saved Lord Darlington from certain death, though there's still some question as to whether or not we'll marry."

"Of course we will," Athena told him firmly. She frowned. "Won't we?"

The uncertain vulnerability filling her eyes was so rare and so raw it speared his heart. "If you'll still have me, then I'm all yours."

Her mouth broadened into a smile that transformed to a grin as she threw her arms around his neck and pulled him close for a kiss. It didn't matter that her parents were standing mere feet away or that the butler had just stepped into the room to inform them dinner was served. Athena didn't care and neither did Robert. The only thing that mattered in that precise moment was that they were back in each other's arms.

"I can have a word with the vicar tomorrow," Robert suggested once they were seated at the table.

"Actually," Athena said, "I'm thinking it might be nice to avoid a big to do for our second attempt."

"We could host something here," her mother suggested, "if you're aiming for a more private event."

"What do you think?" Athena asked Robert.

He loved that she cared about his opinion. From what he gathered, most women tended to take over the wedding arrangements without any thought to their fiancé's wishes.

When he'd planned on marrying Bethany, no one had consulted him about anything. "I think a small affair with only the closest family present sounds perfect."

Athena beamed. "Thank you, Robert."

"And if you're amicable to the idea," he said, "I suggest departing for Darlington House immediately after the wedding breakfast. It won't take more than three hours to reach it as long as the weather holds, and as much as I like Mivart's, I must confess I'm not eager to spend any additional nights there."

"You could stay here," Lord Roxley offered.

"Papa," Athena said, her voice so aghast Robert had to stifle a laugh. "I will not spend my wedding night in the same house as my parents."

"I have to agree with her, dear," Lady Roxley murmured. "It's not really done."

Lord Roxley sighed. "I only meant to tell Darlington that he is welcome."

"Thank you," Robert said, and raised his wine glass toward his future father-in-law. He drank, then glanced at Athena. "Well? What do you think?"

"If we're married by noon and Mama is able to restrain herself to three dishes for the wedding breakfast's menu, then we ought to arrive at our destination by six. Seven at the latest. All in all, I like the suggestion a lot."

Robert couldn't agree more. In fact, the idea appealed tremendously. He was more than ready to make Athena his and could scarcely wait to get her home so they could begin their life together. It pleased him, knowing they were of like minds. It also pleased him to know that she'd never once doubted his love or devotion. When Charles had come to call on him a couple of days ago, he'd told Robert that he'd imagined the worst when Robert had failed to appear at the church, but that Athena's belief in him had never wavered – that she'd been convinced something must have happened to keep him from her. And so it had.

"My sister has matured significantly since you came back into her life," Charles had said. "You have somehow managed to calm her tempestuous nature, which is something I would have sworn wasn't possible."

"I suspect I gave her a dreadful fright. In truth, I've never been so ill before in my life and hope I never shall be again. Athena cared for me with diligence. She's not as irresponsible as you and the rest of your family think."

"No. I'm beginning to gather she's not." Charles's gaze had grown pensive. "I believe she's as lucky to have you as you are to have her. I'm glad the two of you found your way to each other. And I wish you both an endless amount of happiness."

MUCH TO ATHENA'S SATISFACTION, the ceremony was completed one week later in under ten minutes. It was followed by a wedding breakfast consisting of exactly three dishes, of which one was the cake, so the meal was over in record time. And since it was a sunny day, the journey to Darlington House took only a little over two hours. They arrived by six in the evening.

"Although I stand by the apology I gave you when I first came here," Athena said once she'd greeted the servants and Robert had shown her upstairs, "I'm not sorry I prevented you from marrying Bethany. Can you imagine if you had? It would have been awful for me to grow up and fall in love with you only to have you married to someone else while Bethany and Charles loved each other and—."

"I fell in love with you," he murmured to complete her sentence. She occupied the chair adjacent to his near the fireplace in the bedchamber they would now share. The glass of port he'd offered her when they'd entered the room was cradled between her hands. The drink had already produced a pleasant swirl of heat in her stomach.

"Yes. What a tangle it would have been."

"It's a good thing we avoided it then."

"I like to think so."

"And I'm inclined to agree." Reaching out, he took the glass from her and set it aside. With a tug on her hand he pulled her from her chair and toward him, until she landed in his lap. His eyes gleamed in appreciation of her nearness, causing her own body to hum with pleasure. "Everything turned out as it was meant to. They have each other and I have you."

She didn't wait for him to initiate the inevitable kiss. Bold and eager, she closed the distance herself and captured his mouth with her own. Robert's arms tightened around her, drawing her closer until she was pressed against him.

"I could do this forever," she murmured against his skin while trailing soft kisses along his jawline.

"And I would readily allow it."

He sucked in a breath when she pushed her hands under his jacket, and again when her fingers began untying his cravat with deft tugs. Air hissed from between his teeth as he expelled it, prompting her to still.

She leaned back slightly and looked him squarely in the eye. "I know I can be unruly but maybe that's the wrong approach to this? If you'd rather I show more restraint, please say so and I shall strive to—"

"God no." He cupped her cheek. "I love your unruliness, Athena, and frankly, there is no better place for it than here in our bedchamber. If you wish to rip off my clothes, then by all means proceed. I can assure you I will approve."

She grinned, then gasped when he tore the back of her traveling gown wide open – it was the sleeveless one intended to be worn with a shirt underneath. "Robert!"

"I'm only trying to follow your lead," he purred, his gaze so dark and wicked it reached inside and filled her with heat.

Resuming her movements she tugged and pulled while he did the same until he suddenly grinned. "Lord help me. You're once again wearing breeches."

She smirked at him. "Of course. The last time you saw me in them you seemed to like the way they looked."

"God yes." He helped her stand so her gown could be properly removed. His gaze swept her body, which was now clad in creamy buckskin, satin stays, and a perfectly tailored lawn shirt. A grin widened his mouth as he went to work on the laces and buttons. "I do believe we shall have to order several more such outfits for you. To wear in private, of course."

She met his gaze and smiled. "Of course."

Pulling her into his arms, he kissed her while linen and satin floated around them, until they were both completely undressed. A squeal of surprise shot from her throat when he suddenly lifted her into the air and carried her to the bed. His kisses devoured, matching her hunger as he tumbled them onto the mattress. A giggle erupted from within her breast, becoming a sigh of pure pleasure when the palm of his hand swept up over her hip.

"Christ, you're perfect," he whispered while fitting himself between her thighs. "Men really ought to hold hoydens in higher regard."

"We're a very enthusiastic bunch." As if to prove it, she wrapped her legs around him and rolled them over so she was on top. "And I for one am eager to learn. Will you teach me how to be your ideal lover?"

"Yes," he promised in a gravelly tone. His fingertips travelled the length of her spine. She relaxed into his touch and he took advantage, flipping her onto her back when she least expected. A wolfish grin curled his lips, and then he bowed his head to kiss her. "But first, it is my duty to show you the stars."

And so he did, loving her with every kiss and each touch until her soul melded with his.

Epilogue

THE LAKE DISTRICT, Five years later.

Margaret Townsbridge, Viscountess Roxley, sipped her lemonade while her gaze followed the red wooden ball that rolled neatly across the grass. A smile curved her lips when it struck a blue one and her granddaughter, Lilly, emitted a joyful squeal.

"I see," Athena shouted, hands on her hips. "You think you can best me, do you?"

"I'm certainly going to try," Lilly said as she snatched up her mallet and stepped aside so her brother, Lucas, could have his turn.

James and Abigail's children, Henry, Rupert, and Oliver, were participating too, Oliver with the assistance of his uncle William.

In the distance, behind the game of pall-mall, Margaret glimpsed her daughter, Sarah, and her daughters-in-law, Bethany, Abigail, and Eloise. They walked with Sarah's husband, the Duke of Brunswick, and two more grandchildren: Sarah's eldest daughter, Catherine, and Eloise's eldest children, Dominic and Rose.

The rest of the grandchildren, which included Sarah's two-year-old daughter, Mary, and Eloise's three-year-old son,

Max, along with Athena's four-year-old triplets, Penelope, Jenifer, and Hyacinth, plus her two-year-old son, Edward, were being cared for by four nannies.

"This is true wealth," Margaret told her husband, George, as she leaned her head against his shoulder. "A family to love and cherish."

He chuckled lightly, the soft rumble she'd become so familiar with over the years a comfort to all her senses. "When I proposed, I did promise to make you happy, my dear."

"And I have never been more so, my love. With all our children settled and fourteen grandchildren to dote on, what more could I possibly want?"

"I cannot imagine," he murmured in that same low tone that had set her blood on fire the first time they'd danced almost thirty eight years ago. He reached for her hand and threaded their fingers together. "But I'm sure I can think of something."

Margaret's cheeks heated as they invariably did when George showered her with attention. "Tonight perhaps?"

A devilish gleam appeared in his eyes right before he leaned in and kissed her. Laughter and squeals of joy filled her ears while the sun warmed the bright afternoon, and as she answered her husband's caress, Margaret knew they'd been right to encourage their children to choose love above all else.

Thank you so much for taking the time to read the fifth and final book in my Townsbridge novella series. If you enjoyed *An Unexpected Temptation*, you'll definitely enjoy the first book in the series. Grab your copy of When Love Leads to Scandal to discover how it all began.

If you've already read all the Townsbridge stories you should try one of my other series like The Crawfords where three long lost brothers are reunited when their father dies. Each brother ends up romancing one of three female proprietors of an orphanage, only to realize they've had dire consequences on these women's pasts.

There's also Diamonds in the Rough, a rags to riches series in which one character from each book has to figure out how to navigate high society. Start out with *A Most Unlikely Duke* where a bare-knuckle boxer raised in the slums takes lessons in etiquette from the lady next door.

To find out more about my new releases, backlist deals and giveaways, please sign up for my newsletter here: www.sophiebarnes.com And don't forget to follow me on Facebook for even more updates and fun book related posts and on BookBub for new release alerts and deals.

Once again, I thank you for your interest in my books. Please take a moment to leave a review since this can help other readers discover my stories.

And please continue reading for an excerpt from *When Love Leads to Scandal*.

When Love Leads to Scandal

The Townsbridges

Chapter One

Smoky clouds scurried across the London sky as Charles Townsbridge made his way toward the park. He'd gotten into the habit of going for early morning walks years ago when his sister, Sarah, had acquired her first puppy. Their parents, Viscount and Viscountess Roxley, hadn't known about the stray for quite some time, and since Sarah had feared they'd make her get rid of it if they knew, Charles had offered to help. For the next eight years, he'd taken the dog, who'd been named Mozart, out every morning. Because even when his parents were made aware of Mozart's existence and had allowed him to remain beneath their roof, it turned out that Sarah did not have the necessary discipline required at her young age to care for a dog. As she'd gotten older, she'd become more responsible and had suggested to Charles that she should start taking Mozart out in the mornings. He'd apparently revealed how loath he was to part with the task, for she'd only done it once before tactfully asking him if he'd mind continuing.

It was now two years since Mozart had gone off to meet his maker, and yet Charles could not seem to stop taking his walks. They provided him with an excellent start to the day, he realized. The fresh air and movement filled his limbs with the energy required to get things done.

Crossing Piccadilly, Charles was caught by a swift gust of wind. It tugged at his jacket, pulling it tight across his chest before pressing a kiss of cool air to his cheeks. Drawing the brim of his hat down over his brow, he quickened his steps and entered the park where trees bowed their heads in greeting. He was not the only one who'd decided to come here this early. He never was, even though the people at this time of day were sparse and oftentimes only visible at a distance.

Turning onto the path to his right, he took the same route as usual: past the flowerbeds, up the hill, and then down across the grass to the lake. A pair of ducks and their ducklings were bobbing on the water when Charles reached the embankment. He stopped to watch, a smile pulling at his lips on account of the fluffy little creatures swimming along behind their parents.

"My bonnet! Please, please, please, stop my bonnet!"

Charles turned in response to the outcry to find a collection of straw, ribbons, and feathers tumbling toward him. Behind it came a young lady, her white muslin skirts hiked up in her hand to reveal her stocking-clad ankles as she raced down the hill in pursuit. An older woman followed on her heels, albeit at a much slower pace.

Determined to help, Charles jogged to the left and caught the straw bonnet right before the wind carried it into the lake. Turning it over in his hand, he straightened the brim and removed a twig and some leaves from the light blue feathers which appeared to be crushed. The ribbons, a slightly darker blue than the feathers, were twisted together, so he untangled them next before fluffing the feathers with his fingers.

"Goodness me," the young lady panted as she skidded to a halt before him. Her close proximity now allowed him to gauge her age. She did not appear to be more than eighteen. "I scarcely know how to thank you." She raised her chin with a smile, her blue eyes laughing with quiet amusement. Her cheeks were flushed, her hair undone by the breeze in a way that caused one stray lock to fall in her eye while another trailed over her shoulder. Her mouth, he noted, was a perfect combination of rose-petal pink and strawberry cream.

Charles frowned. He'd never compared a feature to something edible before. More odd was how his heart seemed to be hammering about in his chest. Deciding it had to be due to the effort of catching the droopy accessory, he took a deep breath and squared his shoulders.

"There's no need," he murmured, a little surprised by the low timbre of his voice. "I am happy to have offered assistance." He handed the item back to her and watched as she returned it to her head, securing it with the ribbons. "I'm also relieved that I caught your bonnet when I did, or I would have been forced to go for a swim."

Her eyes widened with obvious dismay. "Oh no. I would never have allowed you to do so."

Smiling with every intention of putting her at ease, he told her wryly, "When a gentleman sets his mind to helping a lady, stopping him can be a challenge."

The color in her cheeks deepened, and it occurred to Charles she was blushing, which in turn caused a strange surge of heat to creep under his skin. He cleared his throat and acknowledged the older woman who'd now arrived. She panted loudly and gulped down several large breaths while clutching at the side of her waist with one hand.

Charles addressed her. "I believe a short rest on that bench over there might make you feel better." Stepping forward, he offered her his arm and saw the look of surprise on the young lady's face.

A complicated mixture of emotions shot through him, compiled from the pleasure of doing something useful and the knowledge that many of those who belonged to his set would not offer help to a servant. And that was clearly what this woman was – a maid, most likely, charged with acting as chaperone.

He guided her to the bench and helped ease her down onto the seat. "Better?" he inquired. The chaperone nodded. "Try taking a few deep breaths. Slowly. Not so fast."

She did as he suggested and gradually managed to recover from her exertion. "Thank you, sir. I'm ever so grateful for your assistance."

"As am I," the young lady told him. She'd followed him and the older woman over to the bench and was now standing right beside him.

A jolt of awareness shot through Charles, most likely because she was closer than he'd expected. He turned to face her, his eyes meeting hers and...something indescribable tumbled through him, racing along every vein and snapping at each of his nerves. He'd heard his sisters talk about fated romantic encounters and falling in love at first sight and a slew of other fanciful notions that young girls dreamed of. What he hadn't imagined was that he would ever have cause to wonder if such things were actually possible or if it might one day happen to him.

He did so now, however, for there was something about this woman that sparked his interest. But then the chaperone coughed, and Charles shook his head. He'd obviously lost his mind. There was no such thing as love at first sight, just physical attraction, which was hardly enough to call for courtship or marriage.

With this in mind, he took a step sideways, adding a bit more distance so as not to have his senses stirred even further by the young lady's scent. It was far too sweet to be ignored and only served to tempt him with possibilities.

So he touched the brim of his hat with his hand and addressed both women. "It has been a pleasure, but I fear I must be going now since my family will be waiting for me to join them for breakfast." What reason was there to linger?

"Do you live far from here?" the young lady asked. Her statement was met with a frown and a firm shake of the head from her chaperone. Realizing her error, the young lady bit her lip. "Forgive me. I am often chastised for being too forward, and since you are obviously a bachelor with no ring on your finger and—."

"My lady," the chaperone told her mistress tersely.

Charles smiled. He could not help it. "No need for apology," he said, then touched the brim of his hat once again. "Indeed, I thank you for brightening my morning." And with that he turned away, making his escape while he was still able – before he did something slightly improper, like give her his card. A gentleman did not offer personal details about himself to a lady with whom he wasn't acquainted. A proper introduction would be required. Most especially when addressing what he believed might be a debutante.

BETHANY WATCHED THE tall, broad-shouldered man she'd just met walk away. He'd been handsome. Not classically so, perhaps, but there had been an air about him, a kindness in his coffee-colored eyes that matched his actions. His nose had been straight, his mouth a wonderful indication of what he was thinking, for it had twitched with amusement and curled with pleasure, more animated than any other mouth she'd ever seen.

She sighed, both with happy contentment and some frustration. She could not afford to like this man so well. Not anymore. Not since yesterday afternoon when the Earl of Langdon had come to speak with her father. The offer he'd made for her hand had been precisely what her parents had hoped for, and since Bethany had quite liked the earl and did not wish to disappoint anyone, she'd accepted. Even though there had been no spark.

This spark she'd felt only once in her life. About ten minutes ago when she'd met the man who'd rescued her bonnet. It made her wonder if rushing into a proposal before making her debut had been a mistake. But then she dismissed that idea on the basis of practicality. She was an earl's daughter after all, raised to marry for convenience. Not because some man whose name she did not even know made her heart beat faster. To even consider such a prospect would be insane.

With a groan of irritation directed at the fact that she would likely wonder about the stranger by the lake for days to come, no matter the pointlessness of it, she addressed her maid,

Ruth, who looked quite a bit better now. "Are you ready to return home?"

Ruth nodded and scooted off the bench. They started walking and as they went, Bethany did her best not to think of how perfectly tailored the gentleman's clothes had been. He had good taste, unlike the dandies, whose choice of clothing she found ridiculous most of the time. And then there was his hair. The dark strands peeking out from beneath the brim of his hat had made him look even more dashing. And—

"My lady," Ruth said, interrupting Bethany's thoughts. "I hope you're not cross with me for reprimanding you slightly in front of the gentleman, but it is my duty to protect you and well, you really ought to know by now that you must not be so forward. Especially not with young men whom you don't know."

"Of course. You were quite correct to speak up. And no, I'm not cross with you for it."

"I'm pleased to hear it." They continued a few more paces before Ruth added, "All things considered, he did appear to be a gentleman of good standing, so there's a chance you'll meet him again this evening at the Roxley ball."

"Not that it matters," Bethany said. She glanced at Ruth. "I am now affianced to the Earl of Langdon. Breaking that engagement for any reason would be difficult, but to do so because of a man whose name I don't even know would be terribly foolish."

"And possibly ruinous, my lady, which is why I would never suggest such a thing."

"Just as I would never consider it," Bethany murmured. "Why would I? After all, I've done what every hopeful debutante dreams of doing. I've made a brilliant match with no effort at all on my part. I ought to be thrilled." When Ruth made a *hmm* sound, Bethany amended, "I *am* thrilled."

She and Langdon, or Robert as he now allowed her to call him, had known each other for weeks. Their conversation was amicable, though perhaps a bit reserved. But he did smile when she spoke and had even laughed in her company on occasion. Oh, and he'd also kissed her, which was something, she supposed. Even though it had not been a life-altering kiss, it had been pleasant enough. Certainly, she decided, she and Langdon could be content with each other. And as she walked and the breeze cooled her skin, she accepted that this would simply have to be enough.

WHEN CHARLES ENTERED the ballroom that evening, he greeted the nearest guests politely then sought out his family. Since his sisters, Athena and Sarah, were still too young to attend such events, they had remained upstairs in their bedchambers for the evening. Instead he found his parents and younger brothers, James and William, scattered about. As hosts, his parents were busy conversing with guests, so he decided to approach James instead.

"Do you know if Robert has arrived yet?" he asked after saying, "Good evening," to Baron Garret with whom James was speaking.

"I haven't seen him," James said, "but he usually tends to arrive late at social events, does he not?"

Charles nodded. His friend was never in a hurry to spend time at balls, for he loathed having to dance, but Charles had hoped he'd make an exception this evening. After all, it was three months since they'd last seen each other. Robert had been away in New York and had only just returned yesterday morning. Charles was eager to hear about his travels.

Excusing himself to James and Garret, Charles went to collect a glass of champagne from the refreshment table. The room was already unbearably hot and clamorous from the mixture of conversation and music that seemed to jab at his ears. Charles glanced at the terrace doors. He'd only just arrived and already longed to escape.

Perhaps just for a moment?

His mother would kill him if she found him hiding away on the terrace when he was supposed to be writing his name on dance cards. He considered the row of wallflowers waiting with hopeful eyes directed at each passing gentleman and decided he'd dance with them all this evening. But not until he'd had a chance to cool down a little.

Following the periphery of the room, he reached the French doors leading onto the terrace and stepped out into the fresh night air. A sigh of relief escaped him as a welcome breeze glided over his hair. He took an invigorating sip of his drink and moved further away from the ballroom to where the air wasn't hampered by the wide façade of his parents' home.

A lone woman, silhouetted against the dark garden beyond, was standing near the railing. Charles slowed his progress and prepared to retreat to the opposite corner of the terrace so as not to intrude or risk ruining her reputation by being alone with her.

But then she turned as if sensing him there, and Charles's heart stumbled. It was she, the young lady from the lake, with the eyes he'd never forget and the smile that did curious things to his insides.

She stared at him as if he'd arrived from a dream she'd been having, as if she would happily risk losing other belongings if it would provide an excuse for them to see each other again. Which Charles acknowledged was the oddest contemplation he'd ever had when he didn't know one thing about her. Besides the fact that she was curious, forward, and prepared to abandon decorum, at least to sprint after her bonnet.

"I should arrange for a proper introduction," he said, because that was the only thing that seemed to matter right now – discovering who she was and being allowed to ask her to dance.

She parted her lips as if to respond, but then she appeared to register something and the momentary hint of delight he'd glimpsed was instantly brought to an end. Puzzled, Charles failed to notice the approaching footsteps, but then he felt a hand slap his back and he turned to meet Robert's sparkling eyes.

A rough bit of laughter escaped him. "God, it's good to see you again after all this time. I missed our weekly game of billiards."

Robert grinned. "I've much to tell you, my friend, most importantly perhaps, the fact that I've gotten engaged."

Charles stared at the man whom he knew so well and then laughed. "Truly? You must introduce me at once to the marvelous woman who's managed to tempt you with marriage."

Robert beamed. "It would seem you've already met her." He gestured to the side and Charles followed the movement with the sense that the flame burning bright in his chest was about to be snuffed out forever. The lady from the lake filled his vision, and as he stared into her gorgeous blue eyes, Robert said, "Allow me to present my fiancée, Lady Bethany Andrews."

Grab your copy today to keep on reading!

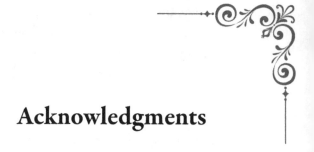

Acknowledgments

I WOULD LIKE TO THANK the Killion Group for their incredible help with the editing, formatting and cover design of this book. And to my friends and family, thank you for your constant support. I would be lost without you!

About The Author

BORN IN DENMARK, SOPHIE has spent her youth traveling with her parents to wonderful places around the world. She's lived in five different countries, on three different continents, has studied design in Paris and New York, and has a bachelor's degree from Parson's School of design. But most impressive of all - she's been married to the same man three times, in three different countries and in three different dresses.

While living in Africa, Sophie turned to her lifelong passion - writing.

When she's not busy, dreaming up her next romance novel, Sophie enjoys spending time with her family, swimming, cooking, gardening, watching romantic comedies and, of course, reading. She currently lives on the East Coast.

You can contact her through her website at www.sophiebarnes.com

And please consider leaving a review for this book.

Reviews help readers find books, so every review is greatly appreciated!

Don't miss out!

Visit the website below and you can sign up to receive emails whenever Sophie Barnes publishes a new book. There's no charge and no obligation.

https://books2read.com/r/B-A-FJPE-WZWHB

BOOKS 2 READ

Connecting independent readers to independent writers.